A SELKIE SEAS PREQUEL NOVELLA

LOSING THE SELKIE'S SKIN

ELLA ROSE

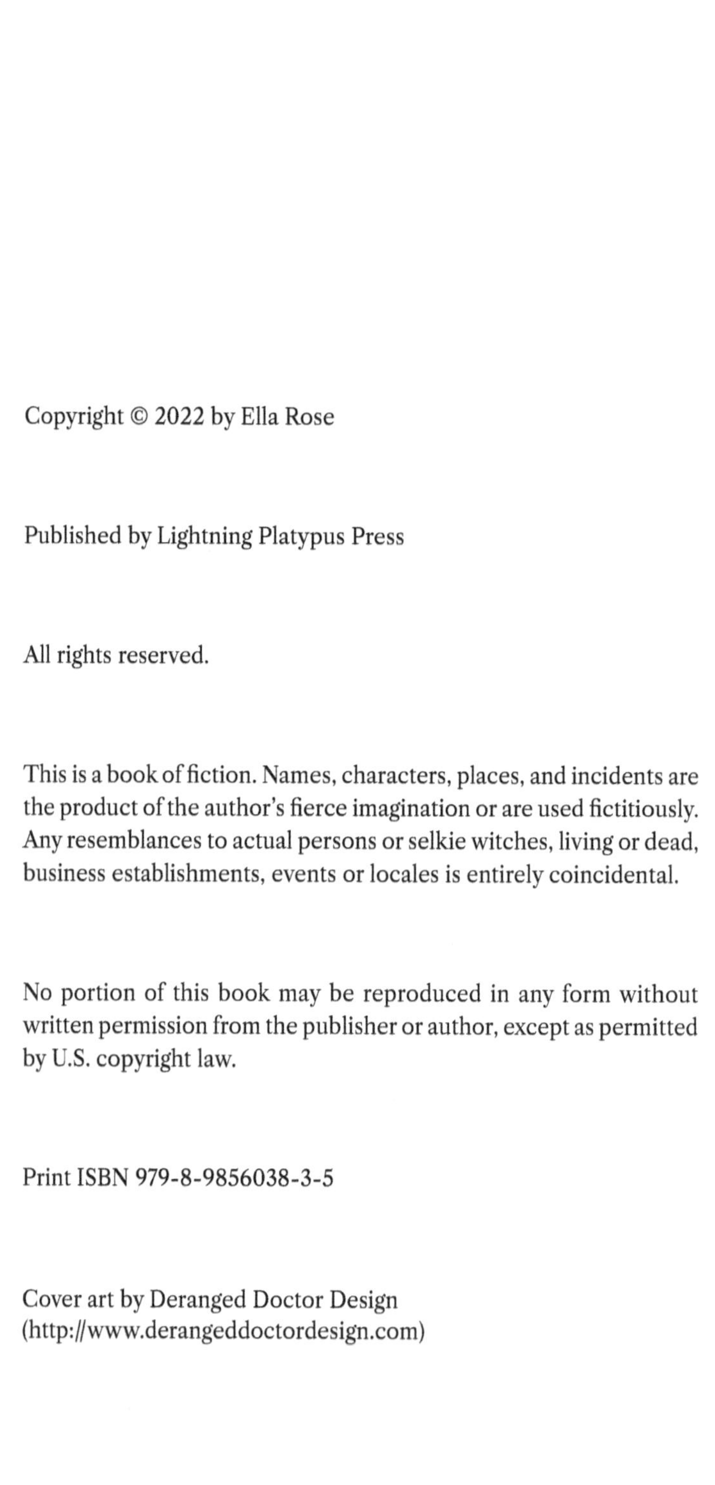

Published by Lightning Platypus Press

Print ISBN 979-8-9856038-3-5

Cover art by Deranged Doctor Design
(http://www.derangeddoctordesign.com)

ALSO BY ELLA ROSE

THE SELKIE SEAS SERIES

<u>Novels</u>

Losing the Selkie's Skin
(A Selkie Seas prequel novella)

Stealing the Selkie's Heart, Book 1
(https://books2read.com/stealingtheselkiesheart)

Saving the Selkie's Heart, Book 2
(available December 2022)

<u>Short Stories</u>
"Watched" in *Worlds Apart* (Dark Rose Press),
M/F selkie flash fiction story (forthcoming)

"The King's Anchor" in
Beyond Atlantis (Dragon Soul Press),
(http://books2read.com/DSPBA)
M/M selkie short story

For Clayton,
who helped me practice

CONTENTS

1. Chapter 1 — 1

2. Chapter 2 — 12

3. Chapter 3 — 23

4. Chapter 4 — 32

5. Chapter 5 — 39

6. Chapter 6 — 49

7. Chapter 7 — 60

8. Chapter 8 — 70

9. Chapter 9 — 82

10. Chapter 10 — 93

11. Chapter 11 — 99

12. Chapter 12 — 106

13. Chapter 13 — 113

14. Chapter 14 — 121

15. Chapter 15 — 130

16. Chapter 16 — 143

17.	Epilogue	149
18.	Free Preview of Stealing the Selkie's Heart	153
Afterword		165
Acknowledgments		167
About the Author		168

CHAPTER 1

1837, ISLE OF SELBANE, in the Hebrides off the west coast of Scotland

Prion lunged upward through the water, letting his flippers dig into the sand of the beach as he emerged from the sea. He paused long enough to quickly use his teeth to unfasten the hooks at his belly, then he reached up with now-human hands to rip his selkie skin from his body. The change was as seamless as the water itself: any onlooker would have seen a seal's head pop out of the water, then a naked human man emerge from underneath it, sweeping the sealskin away like a cape off his shoulders.

Prion stood naked, relishing the warm summer air on his wet body. His stomach was tight, and his erection throbbed painfully. He could almost feel his lover's body underneath him, could nearly taste her lips.

He pulled a necklace over his head and unstrung the cord from the ring that was still cold from the water. Sliding it onto his finger without thinking about it, he wrapped the cord around his wrist with the ease of long practice. Then he flexed his hand against the chill of the ring, and thoughts of delicious anticipation ran through his mind as he let the heavy wet mass of his sealskin fall to the sand. The beach was deserted, as it always was, so he didn't give a second thought as his long legs carried him up the small rise to the dilapidated stone house a few yards away.

She was waiting for him in there, he knew it. As he walked towards the door, which hung crookedly on its hinges, he wondered if she'd found the roses he'd left there yesterday. It had been a trick to ditch his guard, Ronan, to do so, but he'd been thinking about this tryst for days and couldn't wait to see how the female liked what he was planning on doing to her... whatever her name was again. Agna? Or was it Agea? It didn't really matter, he decided as he eased the door open, letting his human eyes adjust to the dim room. She had been willing, and that was all that mattered.

The windows of the ramshackle house lacked any covering, but the fading light of sunset offered little illumination within. Even the holes in the ceiling didn't help much.

He stepped over the threshold and shut the door behind him. "Uh, my lady?" he said. He didn't bother lowering his voice—humans had abandoned the house nearly a decade ago, as far as his reconnaissance told him. That was why he'd chosen it as their meeting place in the beginning—away from the prying eyes of both human- and selkie-kind.

He took a step forward into the room, which was furnished with a single white mattress on a rickety wooden frame. He saw his roses in an earthenware jar on the table next to the bed, undisturbed.

Perhaps she hadn't arrived yet. He'd tried to arrive later than agreed upon to ensure she got there before him, but maybe he hadn't given it enough—

"Stop where you are." He felt the press of cold metal against the tender part of his neck below the jaw.

He grinned in the dim light. "Why, my dear. What a welcome."

The knife tip eased off his neck, and he felt a gentle hand slide over the smooth skin of his naked back. "Lord Prion, you know I couldn't be sure it was you. For all I knew, it was my clan come to claim me." The voice purred in his ear, sending a delightful shiver down his spine. His erection throbbed in anticipation.

He turned and took in his lover. She was tall, almost a head taller than himself, with bright golden hair that trailed over her chest, covering her breasts. Like him, she was naked—their kind rarely bothered with human clothes when it was just them.

She smirked up at him, and he grinned back instinctively. "Someone is definitely here to claim you," he said, letting the desire leak into his voice.

The woman—Agrin! That was her name, he remembered—flipped her hair over one shoulder, exposing one perfect breast, and sauntered past him. He watched as she walked towards the bed, taking in the way her hips rolled as she moved, the graceful curve of her arm as she set the small knife on the bedside table next to the roses.

Everything about her tempted him. She was the perfect distraction from his princely duties, from the responsibilities of the selkie court, and he indulged in similar escapes as often as he could get away with. As the oldest of three brothers, he was next in line to inherit his parents' kingdom, and he had absolutely no desire for it. All the pressure and responsibilities—it was enough to make him scream. All he wanted was peace and quiet, and someone—anyone, really—to help him forget it for a while.

She fingered one rose, and he grinned, imagining the way she would writhe under his touch when he trailed the rose petals over her body. He bit the inside of his cheek to keep from rushing to her on the spot.

"These are lovely." She turned a mischievous gaze on him. "For me?" she said coyly.

Now he let himself stroll towards her, letting all his warrior's training influence the fluidity of his movement. From the way her eyes raked over his body, he knew she was just as hungry for him as he was for her.

"Who else?"

"Oh, perhaps all the lovers you've courted over the years? Rumor has it you like to... dally... outside your clan."

He could detect a hint of jealousy in her tone and grinned at her. "None of them hold a candle to you, my dear," he lied.

She raised an eyebrow at him as he stalked closer. "This is only the first time we've met."

"My point exactly," he drawled. He pointed at the bed. "You. There. Now."

She grinned at him and eased herself gracefully onto the mattress. The bed creaked in warning, and she froze, but Prion ignored it. After the workouts he'd given that bed with others, he knew it would hold a while longer.

"Will this thing hold us?" she asked.

"Probably," he said. "It's the first time I've ever—"

He felt a jolt as if something tugged on an imaginary string behind his navel. "What the seven hells..." Then came the absence, the lack of magical tie that bound him to his sealskin, and he knew it was in someone else's hands. The only way for a selkie to lose their sense of their skin was for someone else to take ownership of it.

He tumbled off the bed and raced to the door, ripping it open so forcefully it bounced on its hinges. He took several stumbling strides out of the house, seeking the feel of his lost sealskin the way a person suddenly blinded might feel for an obstacle in their path. Reaching out with his metaphysical senses, he sought that pull of his skin only to find... nothing. There was no answering pull to tell him which direction the skin was in.

He raced down the beach toward the water, remembering too late how he'd changed, tossed his skin aside on the deserted beach, intent only on the longing in his body for a female's answering touch.

How could he be so careless? The first rule, taught to them as pups, was to protect your sealskin, to always know where it was. Without it, you were lost to the human world, never to change again.

His searching eyes found a hunched figure at the waterline, a dark scaled back bent over at the waist. The strong shoulders bunched as the creature's arms worked furiously over something in its lap.

"Hey!" Prion cried, and the creature jerked upright, whirling to face him with a savage expression.

It was a siren, Prion realized. He saw the scaly features tighten into a scowl as it bared its pointed teeth and hissed at him as he approached. Its noseless face contorted into rage.

"Skinwalker!" it spat at him. "How dare you touch what is mine!" It raised a taloned fist, holding a mass of soggy brown material. "I hope she likes this form you take. It's the last one she'll ever see of you!"

With an awkward twist, unused to moving out of the water, it turned on its fins and dove into the oncoming waves. The brown mass in its hand fell in a heap on the sand.

Instantly Prion felt the magical pull of it again, and he gasped, diving forward on his knees to cradle his sealskin in his lap.

Or at least, what remained of it. As he picked it up, he could feel tears in it that hadn't been there before, and he raised it to his disbelieving eyes to see gaping wounds torn in the oily fur pelt.

"Prion, what happened?" Agrin's voice called from behind him.

He ignored her, too focused on touching the rips in the skin with trembling fingers. He'd never seen damage like this before, not on any selkie's pelt. The tears looked as if they should be bloodied from the damage, gore-covered from the gaps ripped through the blubber and the fur.

Behind him, Agrin skidded to a halt and gasped as she realized what he was holding. "That can't be your skin, Prion. Can it?"

A wordless cry of rage erupted from him, and he clenched his fists in his torn sealskin as he threw his head back and screamed.

From the water on his right, a man appeared, rising naked from the water and pulling a sodden gray sealskin from his own back. "My Lord Prion, what—"

Prion thrust a finger in the direction the siren had gone. "He damaged my skin!" Prion's voice cracked with intensity. "Kill him!"

The naked man clapped a fist over his heart and gave a brief nod. Then he flung the sealskin over his shoulders like a cape and dove into the water. Even as the sea spray rose from his crashing entry, the man was already halfway into his seal shape.

Prion ground his teeth together as his hands worked restlessly over the torn pelt in his lap. His fingers caressed the rips, moving from wound to wound without realizing he was doing it.

Moments later, another selkie rose from the water.

Prion gave him a sharp glance. "Ronan, what news? Did you catch the siren?"

The man called Ronan hesitated, frowning. "It was T'salt, my Lord."

"I know who it was!" Prion shrieked, flinging sand to the side in a burst of rage. "That siren thinks being royalty will keep him from my grasp? He won't be able to breathe through his gills after I rip them from his—"

"Why did he do this?" Ronan interrupted.

Prion's eyes flashed dangerously, but he clenched his jaw instead of raging again. "Because of my... dalliance... with Aislinn." He jerked his chin to indicate the naked woman behind him.

"Agrin!" she cried angrily.

Ronan cast a dubious glance at her, then returned his gaze to his prince. "I don't understand. Why would that matter?"

"He wants me," she said bluntly. "He has approached my mother for a marriage alliance several times. Each time, she politely declined, but he's been providing increasingly decadent gifts to sweeten the deal."

"And what happened this last time?" Ronan asked. "Something must have changed...?"

Agrin's voice was flat when she replied, "I turned him down myself. Said there was no way I'd marry a siren prince, regardless of his gifts." She cast a worried glance at Prion. "I said I was spoken for already, by another of my kind. It was a lie, but I thought that would end his requests."

Prion stared into the distance, his hands working furiously over his torn pelt. "Leave me." His voice was distant, cold.

"My Lord?" Ronan asked hesitantly.

"Not you!" Prion spat. He jerked his head at the woman behind him. "You. Agrin. Leave me. Go back to your own clan."

"But, my Lord, what about—"

"*I said leave me!*" he screamed in fury.

He heard the crunch of footsteps behind him and knew she was returning to the house for her sealskin. He knew she was probably furious, but he didn't care. She was nobody important.

He snatched up the torn sealskin and stalked to the water's edge. He threw the skin over his shoulders like a cape and crouched low on the beach. The ribbons of pelt hung like banners over his pale skin, which peeked through the holes like eyes. He strained visibly, his shoulders shaking with effort, but nothing happened. His hands curled into fists at his thighs.

After several long moments, he straightened, and the skin fell to the ground in a sodden heap. His eyes, staring out at the sea, were far-reaching.

"My parents must know about this," Prion told Ronan. From the corner of his eye, he saw the form of the woman huffily tossing her sealskin over her shoulders and disappearing into the water. "Bring them here as fast as you can."

Ronan clapped a hand to his heart and turned, pulling his sealskin over himself. The change happened before he disappeared under the water, and Prion felt a cold wash of fury come over him.

Land-bound and naked until his parents could come save him. They would be furious. But that paled compared to his situation. Let them be furious—they never approved of his actions, whether or not he acted like a prince. Let them make their comments about his dalliance with another female having gotten him into this situation. He could withstand that, as long as they could fix his problem.

He knew they'd get him out of this mess. They had to.

CHAPTER 2

Leannán didn't know how long he'd been waiting, but when she arrived with his parents and the rest of their retinue, Prion was sitting on the beach with his legs drawn up to his chest, arms resting on his knees, seemingly oblivious to the chill of the ocean breeze against his sun-dried skin.

His father, King Righ, emerged first, unfastening his sealskin in the water and rising like a warrior from beneath it. His long gray hair fell to his waist, with curls of it laying in swirls against his skin. Close behind followed his mother, Queen Mairi. Her long dark hair fell in wet tangles down her body.

Leannán changed into her human form without quite knowing why; she could understand them perfectly in her sealform, but it seemed appropriate to change into the same form as her Queen.

"Prion, what happened?" she heard Queen Mairi ask. She watched as her Queen went to her knees in front of Prion, her hands pressing onto the tops of his.

Prion looked every inch the chiseled man she remembered. Gone was the lanky gangliness of adolescence—this man was made of coral and sun-bleached wood, his youth worn away over the watery years to expose the man beneath. His eyes were bright blue in his tanned face and blazing like snippets of sky between clouds on a sunny day. His face was long, though his dark hair was savagely shorn at his shoulders, hiding the sharp planes of his cheekbones and the strong line of his jaw. His nose was long and straight and his lips were mere slashes in his face.

As handmaid to the Queen, she'd seen him in passing plenty of times as an adult, but this was the closest she'd come in a long time. The sight of him tore at her heart as she watched him hungrily, greedy for whatever bit of him she could feast her eyes on.

The fact that he was her True Mate, the other half of her soul, only compounded her hunger.

"I was... with someone," Prion began, "and I—"

"Who was it this time?" King Righ sighed in a disappointed tone.

Prion shot him an angry glance. "Does it matter? She was innocent in this."

"Where is she now, if she was so innocent?" Queen Mairi spoke up, her voice cold. "Why do we find our son alone on this beach after an attack?"

"I sent her away, back to her clan."

His parents exchanged a look Leannán couldn't see. She was hardly unaware of his trysts—the entire clan knew about his reputation—but his admission still tore at her heart.

When will I stop fawning over this man like a moonstruck pup? she wondered.

"You risk our opportunities for a strategic alliance so you can dally with some other clan's females?" his father asked in a dangerously low tone.

"Can we focus on the real problem here?" Prion cried. "My skin was ruined!" He held up the shredded sealskin from his lap. His mother took it and together she and King Righ worked their hands carefully through it, fingering the tears and rips where the gray blubber shone through like dark lips. Even from a distance, Leannán could see the great holes in it and felt a wash of pity.

"What?" Prion asked. He stood awkwardly. "What is it?"

"We cannot fix this," King Righ said. "And we know nobody who can."

"What do you mean you don't know of anybody? You're the King and Queen of our clan! You know all kinds of magic!"

"Not like this," Queen Mairi said gently. "Our magic only goes so far—minor injuries."

"What about a healer?" Prion demanded. "Surely a healer could—"

"Healers can only mend bodies," King Righ said. "They don't work in magic." His voice dripped with pity.

"Then who can?" Prion cried. Spittle flew from his lips.

A voice spoke up. "A *buidseach* could."

Leannán stood in shock. She couldn't believe the words that had fallen from her mouth. Who was she to suggest mythical solutions to the royal family? She clamped her lips shut, praying to the sea gods that they hadn't heard her.

Prion didn't even look around to see who had spoken. "Those aren't real." His voice sounded empty, tired beyond measure.

Stung, Leannán replied, "They are! And they know more selkie magic than anybody I've ever heard of."

That seemed to catch his attention. Prion's head came up, and he scanned the sea of seal and human faces staring at him from the water.

There.

When he made eye contact with her, she felt her face heat, unnerved at the way everyone else turned to look at her, too. But she straightened her shoulders and met his eyes squarely. "My granddam used to tell me stories about them. She used one to conceive my mother when there was no other chance, and, well, here I am."

King Righ turned to look at her over his shoulder, frowning. His expression was distant, calculating. "And did your granddam ever say where this *buidseach* was?" His voice was soft.

Leannán frowned. "Not exactly. But my dam always told me to stay away from Little Krill Island. Said strange things happen there. It's said to be a place of great and dangerous magic. I'll bet she's there if anywhere."

A look of pity passed over Queen Mairi's face as she looked at Leannán. "My dear," she said, "there is nobody at Little Krill except Amadán, the hermit. And he claims his mother was a *buidseach*. But anybody who goes to see him knows he's the only one there. You must realize this is a farce."

Leannán risked a glance at Prion, expecting to see disdain or anger on his face. But she saw his expression lighten, and she felt a surge of excitement. Maybe he would believe her after all.

Prion stepped forward and put his hand on his father's forearm. His father whirled towards him, and Prion quickly removed his hand.

"Father, if there's a possibility, we have to try. Let me go with a contingent of Anchors and we can find—"

"I'm not sending our warriors away on a hunch to chase a shadow. We need them to protect our clan."

Prion clamped his lips together as if holding back a sharp retort that threatened to burst forth. Instead, he took a deep breath and let it out slowly. "Then let them volunteer. Whoever isn't needed can come help me. I'm sure the necessary Anchors will remain to complete their guard shifts." He scanned the sea of faces with shining eyes. "Who will help me?" he called. "Who volunteers to go on this mission with me, as my protection?"

Silence.

Prion's eyes darted from face to face, and Leannán felt her heart break for him. Nobody could meet his eyes. She couldn't believe it. A member of the royal family was asking for help, and nobody ventured forward to give it?

Finally, she couldn't stand it anymore. In a small voice, she said, "I'll go."

Prion scowled. "Sabin?" he asked to a gray seal next to her. He seemed to have not heard her. The seal ducked its head and looked away. "Ptern?" A bald man standing naked to the waist in the water shook his head mutely.

"I can't believe no one will help me," Prion murmured to himself.

"Can you blame them?" King Righ said in a scornful tone. "You realize that with this act of yours, this *dalliance*, this means war between ourselves and the siren clan. If they don't provide adequate recompense—"

"What recompense can there be for my skin?" Prion cried, throwing his arms wide.

Queen Mairi held up a hand. "They are a proud race. They will not lightly admit fault, even if it was their prince that committed the act."

Leannán felt her stomach roil with anger. How dare they downplay the most important part of this situation? Prion might never be a true selkie again. Their own son!

"Fine. I'll take Leannán and we'll get this sorted out." Prion's tone was as distant as his father's expression, formal and cold. "I'll be back at your side as soon as possible."

Queen Mairi gave him a small smile, but his father just nodded curtly. "See that you do." Then he took his wife's hand, and they turned and pulled their sealskins over themselves. In a rush of waves, the selkies in human form pulled on their skins and changed, hooking the sealskin closed as they dove into the water.

A few breaths later, they were gone, save for Leannán and Ronan.

Prion looked at her. "Are you ready for this?"

She gulped, suddenly nervous: they had been childhood friends. But once he reached his maturity and his parents began piling on his princely responsibilities, they quickly lost track of each other.

"I won't bite," he said with a reassuring smile that looked forced.

"I don't like this," she admitted.

Prion's voice turned silky. "Leannán, precious, why would you pass up the chance for such an adventure? Don't you wish to see the magical caves of lore?"

Leannán frowned and put her hands on her hips. "Not in the slightest."

"You're scared!" he declared. "Aren't you?" Now he sounded like the childhood friend she remembered.

She scowled at him. "I'm not scared of anything! I just don't want to get magicked away by some water sprite, or worse, simply because you're so desperate you can't see how foolhardy this mission is."

Prion scowled back. "If I am desperate, can you blame me?" he snarled. "It's my sealskin! My life! What am I without that skin?" He looked away in disgust. Self-hatred shone in his expression. "No better than a human, that's what," he growled.

Leannán couldn't meet his eyes. She licked her lips nervously. "Look, I'll tell you what I can, but that's it. I'm just a handmaiden. I didn't sign up for—"

Prion glared at her. "Didn't sign up for this? I'm risking everything! And you're the only one who agreed to stand by me."

She frowned, suddenly uncertain in the sheer male force of his presence. Suddenly he was more solid, more real than the other times she'd seen him pass through the court at a distance. "I don't know how much help I'll be. I don't exactly know where to go." It was not lost on her that they'd be embarking on that trip alone together, just the two of them.

Prion strode into the water, catching her by surprise, and grabbed her hands in his. He gazed at her with an earnest expression. "No, but you can show me the way. I'm lost without your help. I'll never find her, if there even is a her to find." He stared at her beseechingly. "Please. I am asking for your help. And only you can help me right now."

Leannán gazed at him uncertainly. She didn't know everything about the stories. But she did remember certain details that he would probably forget. Like the fact that *buidseach* were only ever females and so only females could find them, according to her granddam. Something in the maternal magic that bound them as creators of life made it possible.

He'll never find her on his own, her mind whispered. *He's not the right one.* And in her heart, she knew the voice was right. Besides, she had been planning to leave, though she hadn't known when she would do it—this was just as good a timeline as any. She'd help him, and then go to another clan. She wasn't destined to be with him, anyway.

She closed her eyes in resignation and sighed. She opened them and nodded. "Fine."

Prion's eyes blazed with such intensity that she pulled back, but he pulled her to him, crushing her chest against his as he kissed her. The kiss was deep and forceful and it made her breath catch in surprise and desire.

Prion pulled back and grinned down at her. "You won't regret this."

I'd better not, she thought grimly. The path was much more dangerous than he seemed to realize. *Or that he would let himself admit,* she realized. Prion was nothing if not careful to a fault. At least the old Prion was. He wouldn't rush headlong into a fight without understanding the risks.

Would he?

She had to admit she didn't know. They had grown apart over the years, and despite her knowledge that he was her True Mate, the other half of her that would only bond with him and no other, she didn't really know him anymore. This playboy who shirked all princely duties to run off every chance he got with whatever female turned his head? She had to admit she'd never seen the adult Prion in any high-stress situations. Who could really tell what kind of man he would turn into when under pressure?

But as she watched him give final instructions to his bodyguard Anchor, Ronan, she saw the determination in the set of his strong shoulders, the steely glint of ice in his eyes. He might turn out to be much more formidable than she'd realized. He was a trained warrior, after all, for all his playing at being a Prince.

Maybe they would be successful, she thought, and maybe they wouldn't. But she had to admit, as she watched him dismiss Ronan and turn back to her, watched him prowl towards her with predatory grace, that if anyone could get their sealskin back, it was him.

CHAPTER 3

Prion watched as Leannán led the way into the ramshackle house. The Isle of Selbane, the home to the fishing town of Selbane on the southern side of the Scottish island, was largely inhospitable. He'd chosen this broken-down shack for his trysts, knowing that it was far enough away from the town that nobody would disturb them. Now, he was grateful for its seclusion because it helped him hide his shame from the rest of the clan.

He had known Leannán for almost two decades, had grown up with her, but had never dreamed she'd turn into the beauty he saw before him. She was short, about a head shorter than he was, but with long blonde hair that cascaded like a waterfall down her bare back. She was lean, lithe, and moved on land with the same grace of a seal in water.

Seeing her in the water earlier had been a shock to his senses. He'd known she was in his mother's retinue, but had carefully stayed away, purposefully ignoring her when she was in the room, despite every sense that called to him to look her way. Better she thought him too busy or disinterested to keep contact with her. She had been too important to him when they were younger, the attraction between them too strong as they matured. It was better to distract himself with others who didn't mean anything to him, to forget the way she looked at him...

He tried to focus on the mission at hand, more than a little annoyed that her looks were so distracting in the moment. He watched her as she appraised the inside of the shack, noted the disdainful frown as she spied the roses in the vase next to the bed. She carefully folded her sealskin and set it on the bed.

"Thank you," he began haltingly, unsure of how to talk to her now that they were alone. He fiddled with his torn sealskin, then set it gently on the bed between them.

"For?" she asked coolly.

"Standing up for me when nobody else would." The fact still galled him, but he didn't let that bitterness creep into his voice. She was obviously on the fence about helping him, and he didn't want to influence her in the negative.

The weight of years of distance chasmed between them, and Prion was acutely aware of every time he'd been in her presence and had said nothing. Why had she helped him now when he'd been nothing to her since their teenage years?

I wanted to speak to you.

You look good.

How have you been?

The words lay heavy against his tongue, both necessary and inadequate at the same time. So many things he wanted to say to her. So many things that needed to be addressed, like why he'd suddenly turned away from her as a teenager to pursue princely activities that he'd previously shunned. Or why he'd let the distance between them grow for so long when all he'd longed to do was reach out to her.

In the end, he chose none of these things and instead concentrated on drinking in the sight of her, so near, so close he could almost touch her if he reached out a hand.

She gave a single shrug with one shoulder, the movement graceful and alluring. It made the muscles of her upper back ripple, and he felt a stirring of desire. He turned, not wanting her to see his reaction, and pretended to look around the shack as she was, as if just taking it in, too.

It wasn't a bad place, he admitted to himself. With a little work, it could even be hospitable once more.

Not that he had any inkling of doing that himself, of course. It served its purpose just fine. And once he got his skin repaired, it would continue to serve the purpose he'd designated for it.

Leannán turned to face him, startling him with the directness of her clear gaze. Her eyes were hazel, he realized. Brown ringed with flecks of green around the slitted pupil of their kind. Gorgeous and captivating all at once.

"You wouldn't happen to have anything I can wear around here, would you?"

"I'm sorry?" He'd been so caught up in her eye color he wasn't paying attention to what she'd said.

"Clothes? Here? If I'm going to be around you, I want clothes."

He flashed his most charming grin, the playboy smile that always brought an answering response. "That's never been a problem for most females."

Her frown deepened, and she crossed her arms over her alabaster breasts. "It's non-negotiable."

Prion frowned, feeling his forehead tighten as he did. He tried to avoid that expression when he could—he knew it made small lines appear in his face and he never wanted those age marks, as they were unattractive. Then he smoothed his expression and gave a tight smile. "Of course."

He walked over to one corner of the room, where he kept a few spare sets of clothes, and pulled out a loose cotton shirt with small mother-of-pearl buttons down the front and a pair of drawstring pants. He tossed them on the bed near her. As she pulled them on, he fought the wave of disappointment he felt as the fabric of the clothes swallowed her pale skin.

She finished, then put her hands on her hips. "Now you."

"I'm sorry?" he repeated, nonplussed. "I don't like clothes."

"Well, I'm not going to talk to you without them. I don't want to see you naked."

He drew back, stung. It had been a long time since he had been undesirable to a female. Decades, in fact. And how to see that detached look on her face when she said it... He opened his mouth to retort, but she pointed to the pile of clothes at his feet.

"Please? It will make me more comfortable." He noted a strange blush creeping up her cheeks, then discarded the idea as he had no clue why his nudity would give her that reaction.

"Fine," he spat, as he bent to gather the clothes. "But I'm doing this under duress."

She snorted, which he ignored.

As he pulled on his pants, she asked, "What's that ring you wear? Our kind rarely wear human jewelry."

"It's not human jewelry," he said, glancing down at the ring. It was platinum, a white gold ring with a square, flat head with rounded edges. A large embossed L sat atop it, with silvery scroll-work ringing the edges. "It's my grandsire's. He gave it to me right before he died."

"What does the 'L' stand for?"

"Liath Clann. My grandsire believed your clan was the most important thing a selkie had, that without it, you had nothing. He tried to teach the rest of us the same."

"Your brothers?"

He pulled a light cotton shirt over his head and nodded. "Andara seems to get it, but Trian? He's still got a lot to learn."

Once he was clothed, grimacing at the itchiness of the fabric against his skin, he pulled over a rickety-looking wooden chair and flounced down in it. He affected a posed slouch and looked at her. "Now what?"

She looked around for another chair, then stood awkwardly in place when she didn't see one. For the first time, she looked uncertain. "Now what *what*?"

Prion spread his arms wide. "What do we do now? You're the boss of this expedition. I don't know how to find the selkie witch—"

"*Buidseach*," Leannán corrected.

"—I don't even know what she looks like," Prion continued as if she hadn't spoken, "She could have horns and tentacles and whatnot for all I know. And I don't know how to get to her as I am *stuck*"—he waved an arm up and down to indicate himself—"in this human form for now. So how do you propose we go about this effort?"

Leannán frowned, pinching her lower lip between her fingers as she thought. "You couldn't swim, that's for sure," she said, thinking aloud. "And we need to get out to Little Krill Island to see… who was it your mother said lived out there? The hermit?"

"Amadán," Prion supplied in a bored voice.

"Right, him. He can probably tell us how to find a *buidseach*. But she's bound to be water-based, as a selkie, so we'll need to travel by water… We'll have to charter a boat." Her eyes lit up as she warmed to the idea. "Yeah! That's it! We'll hire a human to sail us to where we need to go."

Prion snorted and rolled his eyes. Leannán's face fell. "And how do we convince this human to take us? Should we explain what we are and what we are trying to do?" His voice dripped with derision and bitterness.

Leannán pursed her lips, obviously fighting the urge to wilt under his contempt. She straightened her shoulders and lifted her chin. "We pretend to be together. Say that we are traveling on our honeymoon to see the world. We have a special place in mind, but we will make it worth his while to take us."

"And how will we pay for this?"

"With your parents' gold."

With raised eyebrows, Prion stared at her. He couldn't believe the audacity of what she was saying: spending the King's money without asking first, assuming they'd help after turning their son away. But he knew his mother, if nothing else, would want to help him. And they had plenty of treasure with which to bargain. He nodded his head thoughtfully. They had to help him.

Without it, they were sunk.

"Ok," he drawled. "Ok. And where do we find this charterman?"

"In Selbane." Leannán jerked her chin to show the direction of the town. "We can hire some fishing captain, make it well worth his effort. Your parents will help us, right?"

"Of course they will!" Prion said with gusto, though inwardly he wasn't quite certain he wasn't lying. "They'll help. They have to."

"Then I will go to them and get the money. We head out at dawn. We need to get started as quickly as possible."

Prion agreed wholeheartedly. The sooner he got his skin repaired, the sooner he could get past this nightmare and on with his normal life.

He paused. Maybe this was a second chance, one he certainly didn't deserve, but perhaps could use to his benefit. He cleared his throat, "Leannán, precious," he began, but stopped when her face closed on itself like a door slamming shut.

Inwardly he kicked himself. Why couldn't he speak to her like they used to, like they were equals? Back before he had forced distance between them, they had been inseparable, best friends. He had told her everything, had laid his heart bare about a thousand things that seemed important at the time. But now? Now he couldn't see to drop the affected speech, the winsome persona he'd developed over time and had perfected on countless females.

But they'd all treated him as the Prince of Liath Clann, swooning over his every word, obeying his every whim. And the Leannán he remembered had never treated him as anything less than just...Prion. In the face of that, he found he suddenly had no idea where to begin.

When he just stared at her, she gave a small frown and turned. "I'd better go."

He watched as she pulled her sealskin over her shoulders like a cape and strode with purpose towards the door. He let her go alone, not bothering to walk her to the water's edge, as he knew he probably should. But he couldn't bear to watch her shift. It was too painful.

Instead, he sat in the uncomfortable chair and plotted. "It's only a matter of time," he murmured to the empty room. "Just a matter of time."

CHAPTER 4

FINDING A CAPTAIN, HOWEVER, proved to be harder than it looked. They entered the town of Selbane in late afternoon, as the ships were returning to the dock for the day. They wandered the walkway along the edge of the docks, taking in the rows of tall fishing vessels and the bustle of fishermen and crewmen as they prepared to unload the day's haul from their boats.

"How do we find the right one?" Leannán whispered to Prion. She was playing the part of a new wife, clutching his arm as they strolled, trying to appear nonchalant as they inventoried their options.

"We'll have to just pick one and go with it," Prion said in a low voice. His voice was tight, with nerves, and Leannán wondered if it was because of being this near humans—which, truthfully, unnerved her a little, too—or being so long in his human form. She didn't mind it, the itch like saltwater dried on the skin that urged her to don her skin and leap back into the water. But she held it at bay and struggled to get her flipping stomach under control. Prion had warned her not to look too nervous, lest they appear weak and get taken advantage of. So she straightened her shoulders and tried to gaze at him lovingly and still eyeball the ships for the likely candidate.

"Oi!"

They paused their feigned strolling and turned towards the call. A man leaned over the prow of one of the docked ships. Leannán noted it was named *The Hellion*. A young man in his twenties leaned over the railing and was smiling at them with a predatory look. "You two aren't looking like you're from around here. Looking for anything in particular?"

"A charter ship," Prion called back in a strong voice. Leannán was proud to hear that none of his nerves showed in his voice. "We are newlyweds and have need of a ship to take us on a journey."

"How long a journey?"

"As long as it takes," Prion muttered to Leannán. Then, raising his voice to be heard, he called back, "A few days, we think. Maybe a shade longer."

"Can you pay?" the man asked. Leannán didn't like the look of him. Too greedy, too arrogant.

She tugged on Prion's arm. "I don't think this is the right one," she said in a low voice, but Prion shrugged her off with an irritated glance.

"I know what I'm doing," he growled at her. Then, to the man, he said, "We can pay. How much do you charge?"

"Twenty gold pieces," the man said. He hiked his foot up so he could rest his elbow on his knee as he scowled down at him.

"I'll take you for fifteen," another voice called. They turned their heads and saw a man leaning over the rail of the ship docked next to *The Hellion*, called *The Tamed Tempest*. This man was a few years older and weathered around the eyes with skin that had obviously seen much of the ocean water.

They turned to the first man, who was scowling at the other captain. "Don't you try to take my catch today, Breck!" he warned, pointing a finger.

The man called Breck shrugged. "Just trying to keep my prices competitive, Adair. Don't you know how business works? Better product for less money, that's how you keep a customer. You never learned that."

"Better product, my ass!" Adair boomed. "My *Hellion* can outsail the *Tempest* any day!"

"You couldn't outsail the *Tempest* from a teapot," Breck scoffed. "What about last month's haul, huh?"

Adair's face darkened. "That was a bad month for everyone, and you know it."

"Wasn't for me."

"Because you have some honey hole nobody knows about! It's not fair—"

"Nothing seems fair when you're losing, Adair," Breck interrupted with a serene smile.

Adair seemed apoplectic. He opened his mouth to reply, his face dark with anger, but Prion turned to Breck. "For fifteen gold, you can have us."

Adair appeared to deflate. He gazed back at them with a weak sort of confusion, then turned a venomous glare on Breck. "Mark my words, Breck. Someday I'm going to be mayor of this town, and then you'll be sorry you crossed me."

Breck gave a dismissive wave of his hand as he turned curious eyes on Prion and Leannán. "So tell me more about this honeymoon spot of yours."

"Can we come aboard first?" Prion asked in an irritated voice. Leannán wondered if he was tired of bending his neck upward to speak to the captain.

"Of course, of course!" Breck laughed, and waved them to the side of the ship where a ramp connected the ship to the dock. As they passed the front of the ship, Leannán noticed a large seal painted on the nose, its body arcing in a graceful dive. The sight of it gave her a small thrill of excitement, and she knew they had found their ship.

As they walked up, Leannán realized the *Tempest* was rather large, sporting two large sails that rose to the sky like banners. "Your ship is impressive," she told Breck after shaking his hand.

He grinned. "Thanks, lady." He gazed around the ship with a fond smile. "She's a wily bitch sometimes," he said ruefully, "but one of the best luggers on the water." He jerked his chin at *The Hellion* behind them. "A sight better on the water than that Skaffie." Leannán stared at him. Lugger? Skaffie? None of those words meant anything to her, but she figured they were unimportant to their mission.

"And how many men comprise your crew?" Prion asked thoughtfully, gazing around the ship. They had passed no men hovering around the ramp and saw none on the ship's deck.

"About 6 of the hardest-working men this side of—"

"We just want you," Prion said in a hard voice, looking Breck full in the eyes.

Breck's affable smile fell away as his brows raised in surprise. "That's not possible. It takes a minimum of two people to—"

"That's fine. Two of you, no more."

The beginnings of a scowl crept across Breck's lined face. "Now see here, this is my ship and I'll not have—"

"We'll double the amount," Leannán broke in, fighting to keep the desperation out of her voice. She had a good feeling about this man, cocky as he might be, but at least he wasn't full of bravado like his companion Adair seemed to be. She had a feeling that the *Tamed Tempest* was their way to the *buidseach*, and she couldn't let the opportunity pass them by.

Prion shot her an irritated glare, but she gripped his arm so hard he flinched. But thankfully, he stayed quiet. They both watched Breck, waiting for his reaction.

A series of emotions flew across Breck's face at her words: shock, anger, and finally a calculated wariness. "You'll double the amount if it's just me and Jack?"

Prion shrugged. "Whomever you choose. But we keep this expedition small."

Breck scratched his head with a doubtful look on his face, then nodded. "All right. We'll do it your way. But you pay half up front—"

"Half?" Prion squawked angrily.

"—and half when we dock back here at the end." Breck's face still held a trace of doubt, but his eyes were direct and strong when he added, "Or no deal."

Prion worked his mouth as if he'd tasted something sour. Leannán looked back and forth between the men, then squeezed Prion's arm. "Deal."

Breck nodded at her, then cocked his head, waiting for Prion's acknowledgment. Prion nodded, looking disgruntled, and the men shook hands. Prion fished out a small coin purse and handed it over. Breck pocketed the purse without glancing at it, and Prion held out a hand.

"Wait, don't you want to count it? You huma—" Leannán pinched his arm. "Fishing captains," Prion quickly amended, "aren't known to be the trusting types."

But Breck just grinned at him. "You're about to be out in my element for multiple days. If I find out you shorted me, I'll just find an island and leave you there." He nodded at Leannán in dismissal, then pushed past Prion towards the ramp. "And we sail at first light tomorrow. Be ready with your map."

And just like that, he was gone, down the ramp and along the dock towards the main part of town.

Prion and Leannán looked at each other.

"Do we trust him?" Leannán asked in a low voice. She felt very exposed this high out of the water, where the wind from the ocean blew a salty cool breeze across her face.

Prion continued to gaze after Breck. "We don't have much of a choice, do we?" he returned softly.

CHAPTER 5

THE DECK BELOW THE *Tamed Tempest* wasn't anything special: two furnished rooms, one with a set of bunk beds built into the wall, and a cargo hold. Captain Breck graciously offered his room to them to stay in, while he bunked with his second-mate, Jack, in the other room. Jack Anderson turned out to be a small, wiry man with a shock of curly red hair set beneath a worn fabric cap. His pants were cut off at the shins and frayed and patched at the knees, as if they had seen better days.

But the Captain's quarters were clean and well-furnished. The bed was large enough that Prion figured he and Leannán could both fit in, though she'd been upset at the prospect.

"There is no way I'm sleeping with you in that," she said when they dropped their meager bags containing a few days' clothes and their sealskins, carefully wrapped in thin blankets to hide from prying eyes.

Prion's eyes twinkled as he grinned at her. "Where else would you sleep? The floor?" He gestured to the table next to the bed. "Besides, he even stocked us with a bouquet of roses for the newlyweds. How sweet!"

Leannán looked thunderous, but he just smiled. It wouldn't bother him at all to sleep in such cramped quarters, he'd slept in worse, and it certainly wouldn't hurt to be pressed so close to Leannán for an entire night.

And who knew what might come from that? he wondered to himself. He cocked an eyebrow at Leannán, who was staring horrified at the roses, and excused himself to join Breck on the top deck.

It had surprised the Captain to find out where they were headed. "Little Krill Island?" he asked. "There's nothing there but rocks and regret. Why would you want to go there?"

"There's a man there," Prion said, choosing his words carefully. "A very, *very* distant relative we wish to visit. It will be a quick stop, just enough to say hello. And then we can be on our way."

"To where?"

"What?" Prion asked weakly.

"What are we going after that?" Breck asked, annunciating the words slowly as if Prion couldn't understand them.

"Oh, well..." Prion's mind raced, but he couldn't think of anywhere else to say. "After that, we'll just see. We might go where the wind takes us for a while."

Breck stared at him, nonplussed. "You just want me to sail around? To nowhere in particular?"

Prion frowned. "I'm not sure if you've ever been married before, Captain Breck—"

"It's just Breck out on the water."

"Breck, then. But we are less concerned with the destination, and... ah... more concerned with the journey, if you get my drift." He waggled his eyebrows at Breck, who grinned back.

"I've a wife of my own," Breck admitted. "Pretty thing. And I remember how it was between the two of us. Couldn't keep our hands to ourselves half the time." He smiled wistfully, and Prion gave him a calculated glance.

So the human was a romantic. That was good to know. Perhaps that would come in handy in the future.

He pasted an affable grin back on his face, then clapped Breck on the shoulder and went back below-deck.

"I've managed to put him off for a bit," he said as he closed the door behind him. "But eventually, we'll have to figure out where to go after visiting Amadán."

Leannán sat on the edge of the bed, pulling her hair over one shoulder to stroke it absently. The gesture left her neck exposed on one side, giving Prion a good look at how slender and pale it was. *Perfectly kissable*, he thought.

He strolled casually over to the bedside table and pulled a rose from the vase.

"Maybe we won't have to go anywhere after Amadán," Leannán was saying in a hopeful tone. "Maybe his mother really *was* a *buidseach* and we'll meet her and she can—"

Prion slid the silky head of the rose down the side of her neck.

Leannán jumped to her feet, whirling around to face him. "What in the seven hells do you think you're doing?" she demanded.

Prion grinned at her, letting all the lust and desire bleed into his eyes. "Just enjoying myself."

"Well, do it without touching me," Leannán retorted, putting her hands on her hips.

"Leannán," Prion chided, looking at her from underneath his lashes. "Doesn't it get lonely being handmaiden to my mother all the time? Always waiting on her needs, never fulfilling your own?"

"What do you know about whatever needs I have to fulfill? You haven't spoken to me in ages."

"But I've kept tabs on you," Prion admitted. He felt a rush of satisfaction at the surprise on her face. If only she knew exactly how much he knew about her from over the years. "Oh, yes. My father and I keep tabs on all the handmaidens privy to my mother's secrets. We have to make sure we have trustworthy advisors. And can you imagine my surprise to find that the lovely Leannán is quite solitary? No suitors. No mate. No dalliances."

Leannán's eyes flared in indignation. "No, the dalliances are *your* area of expertise, not mine."

Prion stalked towards her, noting the sudden dilation of her pupils, the flaring of her delicate nostrils as he approached. She backed away, hands reaching blindly behind her. He pressed forward, letting all his frustration and power focus with single-minded intensity on the changes in her breathing, the quick fluttery breaths that made her breasts rise tantalizingly fast, the pulse that fluttered like a bird at the base of her neck.

He stepped forward until her back hit the wall of the cabin, then pressed ever so slowly closer until their chests touched. "You want me, Leannán. It's plain to see. And I'd be a fool not to want you."

"You've never wanted me," she panted, her panicked eyes fastened on his lips.

He dipped his head, bringing their faces closer and closer until his lips brushed hers. "I want you now," he whispered.

Her response was immediate. She hurtled herself at him, hands pressed to either side of his face as she kissed him with such intensity that it took his breath away. He felt the smooth brush of her tongue across his lower lip and moaned. She tasted salty, briny like the sea in a way that was immediately comforting to him. He wanted more.

His hands slid down the sides of her body, feeling the firmness of the muscles along her ribs, the plumpness of her buttocks as he cupped them in either hand. She moaned into his mouth, and he felt the sharp pang of desire race through him.

"On the bed," he managed, pulling back slightly. But she crushed her mouth on his once more, so he twisted, pulling her with him so that they stumbled towards the bed, crashing down on it with her underneath him.

Using all his skills, he deftly pulled her clothes from her body, tossing them to the floor with ease of practice. Then he pulled back long enough to shuck out of his own clothes, pulling them off as quickly as he did his sealskin when he changed. For a moment, he loomed over her, gazing down at her naked body.

She stared up at him hungrily, her eyes feasting on the planes of him. But he wanted to feel her skin against his, feel her pale flesh hot as fire against him, wanted to sheath the erect part of him deep inside her warmth and pulse into her until they both shattered from the impact.

He paused, his breathing ragged, and leaned over her to pluck another rose from the vase. "Close your eyes and lie back," he instructed.

With a dazed half-smile, as if she couldn't believe this was actually happening, she complied, laying back on the single pillow in a way that let him get an eyeful of her perfect, lean body. Her breasts were like two apples, pert and round and perfect for his hands.

He crawled on his hands and knees towards her. He straddled her legs, and leaned forward, careful to let his erection brush the tops of her thighs. Her lips parted in anticipation, but she kept her eyes closed, as he'd commanded.

He drew the rose across her lips like a painter would a paintbrush, letting the silken petals slide down her chin and neck, and between her breasts. She squirmed, smiling, then stilled as he lifted the rose again.

"I love watching you," he said.

The rose slid down her stomach to the sensitive area between her legs. She wriggled, grinning, as it caressed her most intimate area.

"More," she gasped, then moaned in disappointment as the rose withdrew. Moments later, she felt his head slide between her legs, his hair rough against her inner thighs, and his tongue lapped at her.

"Yes!" she cried, as his tongue dipped between her slick folds. He nibbled her clitoris, and she cried out again in pleasure.

"You are such a delicacy," he murmured against her.

"I can tell," she murmured. His tongue darted inside her again as his hand crept up to caress and pluck at her nipple. She writhed under his touch, moaning his name as her fingers curled into the hair at the base of his skull, pulling him closer to her with every motion.

She finally cried out as the waves of sensation engulfed her, climaxing around his tongue as he quickly slid his fingers inside her, thrusting in time with her shudders.

Then, as he felt the creeping rise of desire curling within his own stomach, he leaned back until he towered over her on his knees.

"Put me in your mouth," he said, his eyes dark with dirty promises.

She gripped the base of him, brought him towards her, then slowly took him into her mouth.

He filled her mouth with his thickness and she moaned against him, delighting when he moaned back in response and clutched the back of her head. His fingers dug into her scalp as she circled the base of him with her tongue. The rose trailed a silky path down her check, resting against the bulge of him in her mouth.

She purred around him and his fingers clenched.

"Do that much more and I won't last very long," he said through clenched teeth.

She pulled back long enough to say, "That's fine with me," and went back down on him again, sucking and pumping with her one hand around the base of him while she flicked her tongue across his tip.

"I'm close," he ground out, and she pulled back. He shifted so that his body covered hers and situated himself firmly between her legs.

He slid inside her and she cried out, still sensitive from moments before. But as he pumped in and out, she rose to meet him thrust for thrust.

"Oh, gods, Leannán!" he panted.

Her fingers raked down the thick muscles of his back as he rode her, panting and gasping as he climaxed, the wave of it crashing over him completely. Moments later, as he slowed, she clenched her legs together around him and cried out herself.

For a moment, Prion felt an echoing sense of himself, two heartbeats beating in frantic, out-of-sync rhythm, one right after the other; two sets of lungs heaving for breath that was separate from the audible gasps rung from himself and Leannán. Then the sensation faded, leaving him feeling just himself and the exhilaration threading through his body, making him feel lighter than before.

He knew what that ghosting sensation meant. He wasn't the heir to the selkie court without knowing a few important things himself, most especially about the lore of their kind. Oh yes, he knew what the pulsing heartbeats meant and inwardly he reeled.

Slowing, he leaned down so that his forearms held his weight. Still, the pressure of him against her chest was comforting, his warmth radiating from him like a furnace. She smiled up at him.

"That was wonderful," she said with a languid smile.

He kissed her forehead, realizing that he had never had better. In all the females he'd been with, none had brought him so quickly, had wrung him out so completely. Being with her was like coming home, and now that he'd felt the start of the True Mate bond flaring to life between them, he knew nothing would ever be the same.

CHAPTER 6

PRION HAD FALLEN ASLEEP, but Leannán was wide awake. How could she have done that? It was asinine to believe his words, that he truly wanted her, and it was certainly not the way she wanted him, but... Oh gods, had it been worth it.

She lay there, feeling the warmth of him against her side, listening to the deep bellows of his breathing, rhythmic and slow. The True Mate bond had flared wildly inside of her as she climaxed, feeling the doubled sense of Prion's body, though she knew it wouldn't have brought the telepathic connection of True Mates unless they'd come together. But it was still stronger between them, and it shocked her that he didn't seem to notice it.

Unless he did and was just ignoring the signs? That was possible, given his regular habit of ignoring things that didn't fit his purpose. And strong feelings of attraction were commonplace to him—he may not realize the depth of his reactions as being that of proximity to his True Mate. He probably just passed it off as simple lust.

The thought galled her. That she was only another pawn in his game, just another face that he wouldn't remember in the morning. Yet, he had cried out her name. That had to mean something, right?

She had known, since she was a teenager, that he was her True Mate. Had known it deep in her bones with the resonating frequency of struck metal. She still remembered seeing him the next day, the day after she started her bleeding, and how looking at him had brought on a double-sense of two heartbeats and two sets of lungs working out of sync with each other. For a moment, her vision blurred, and she saw herself as he saw her, lanky, beautiful, and familiar. Then the moment passed, and she'd been back in her own self, feeling her own pounding heart beating in her flushed cheeks.

For her, the moment had been a revelation, a thrilling sense that the mystical sense her dam had told her about was true. She had longed to tell him, but she'd been scared, so scared of what he would say.

A week later, he'd moved to a different part of the court, his own schedule changing to mean more studies, more training, more weapons mastery.

They had never really spoken past that, and she regretted never having sought him out to tell him herself.

But now. If fate had brought them together in this way, surely that was a sign that they were meant to seal the bond.

Prion rolled over in his sleep and slid an arm over her ribs, pulling her closer.

"Leannán," he murmured against her shoulder and sighed.

She felt a thrill of excitement. He had to feel the connection between them. He just had to.

But she was under no delusions that this meant anything would change between them. The thought made her lips twist. He would still turn back to his old ways once they repaired his skin—there was no reason for him not to. Once all was fixed, this would be just a bad dream for him, and she would be a nobody once more.

"But I've kept tabs on you."

He could continue keeping tabs on her... after she had moved on to another clan. It had been the plan for a while now, as she'd pined for him, watching him ignore what he was destined for, watching him flirt and play with every female that moved past him. It broke her heart daily, and she couldn't take it anymore. She'd not had a plan about when she'd do it, at least not until he'd asked for volunteers to help him. That had solidified her timeline in her head, and now she knew there was no going back.

Regardless of how intimate they got, however close she wanted to pretend they were, True Mate bond or no, she knew, deep down, there was no hope for them to be together. There never had been.

She sighed and felt a tear trickle down the side of her cheek. All her hopes, dashed. Her secretmost dreams, shattered. She would transfer to another clan after all this was over and leave him behind to live his life the way he wanted. She just couldn't watch it happen anymore.

The faster we get through this, the better, she thought to herself.

She rose and dressed quickly, ignoring the distressed moan he gave when she slid out from beneath his arm. The sound of it tugged at her heart, but she pushed it away. Amazing as it had been, she would have to make sure this kind of thing never happened again. She would cherish the memory and pine for it no longer. She was determined not to.

So she made her way up to the top deck, searching for Captain Breck.

Instead, she met Jack on the stairs, coming down as she was going up.

"Oh-ho!" he exclaimed with a wide smile. "My lady." He dipped his cap in greeting. His hair was tousled from the wind, and he smelled of salty air and open water.

She inhaled, savoring the scent. "Jack, good morning. Is Breck up there?"

"At the helm, lady. You can find him at the bow of the ship."

She hesitated, frowning. "Bow?"

Jack's smile turned rueful. "Toward the front, nearest the nose."

"Ah, thank you." She made to move past him, but he hesitated, pulling his cap off and pressing it to his chest.

"My lady, I have to say something. I feel it's important for you to know." She raised her eyebrows, and he seemed to gather his courage to speak. "This island you're headed to, Little Krill. It's known by another name, did you know?"

She shook her head. "That's the only name my... people... know it as." She caught herself before she said "my clan."

Jack glanced over his shoulder, towards the top deck, then back at her. "It's known to sailors as Little *Kill* Island. Because it's treacherous."

"Is it just hard to sail?" she asked, curious.

Jack hesitated, then said, "Not just. I mean, there are rocks that surround it, making it nigh impossible to dock on-site. But there are... rumors."

Leannán felt a twinge of unease. "What kind of rumors?"

"Of things happening. Bad things. There's rumor of bad magic hanging about the place. Nothing ever goes right when a ship passes close to there."

This man was obviously uncomfortable speaking of such things to her, and she had to commend him for working up the courage to mention it at all. She wondered if the bad magic was some sort of spell the *buidseach* used to keep people away. If so, it could only mean they were on the right track.

She forced a smile, despite the warring feelings of excitement and dread churning in her stomach. "I'm sure we'll be fine. Captain Breck—"

"Is a fine Captain, m'am," Jack hurried to add. "One of the best I've sailed with. But I would hate for something bad to happen on your honeymoon, lady. These are supposed to be good times, not ill." He stared at her in earnest worry, and she felt a rush of gratitude. He was a simple human worried about things out of his league, but he was trying to help them have the best possible trip.

If only he knew what we're really after, she thought.

She smiled at him and placed a hand on the arm holding his cap. "Jack, I appreciate your worries.

But we are adamant about visiting my family on that island. We can't pass up this chance. We will be fine, don't worry. My husband is... very adept. He can take care of the both of us there. When do you think we'll be there?"

Jack forced a strained smile, but she could tell he wasn't entirely convinced. "Today, m'am. In a short while. We sailed while you slept."

She nodded and looked at him expectantly, wondering if he would try to convince her again to turn back. It was to his credit that he crushed his cap back on his head, nodded at her, and stepped past her without another word.

She glanced after him, watching until he disappeared into the cargo hold, then made her way up the stairs. A gust of wind hit her face as she breeched the deck, and she took a deep breath. She would never tire of the sea air, the freshness and wildness of it as it skimmed the open water and carried essences of salt and freedom to her skin. If she had to live as a human, she thought, she'd want it to be near the ocean, where she could feel its nearness and untamed air every day of her life. To be without it was to be without part of her soul.

The idea brought a flash of pity for Prion. To be this near the water and unable to change to swim in it must gall him every day. Thankfully, they were closer to fixing the issue than they had been before.

And closer to parting, she thought with a flash of sadness. Then she straightened her shoulders, pushing the thought aside. That line of thinking would do no good. *Focus on the now,* she told herself. *The rest will follow.*

She found Breck at the wheel—near the front of the ship, as Jack had said—gazing out along the horizon with a far-reaching look. He glanced over, surprised, as she approached him from behind.

"Morning," he said with a nod. "I trust you slept well?"

"As well as I could," she said wryly, thinking of Prion's hands on her body.

Breck chuckled, and she realized he took her answer in a different way. She blushed, but he was looking out over the water instead of at her and didn't see it. "We'll be there soon." His voice was low and gruff, as if the sea air had weathered his voice as well as his skin. But there was a kindness to it that she noted and appreciated. "I suppose Jack had words with you down below?"

She looked at him, surprised, then realized they must have been discussing it while she and Prion were below deck. "He did."

Breck nodded as if this were of grave importance. "And you're determined to press on, then?"

"I'm up for the challenge if you are," she said with an arced eyebrow.

He glanced at her with a sideways grin and eased the wheel to one side. He raised one arm and pointed off to their right. "Then that's where we're headed."

She followed the direction of his finger and saw a small island in the distance, closer than she expected. They were very close now. Even from this distance, she could see the rocks jutting from the surrounding water, with the waves splashing white caps of foam into the air as they crashed against the outcroppings.

"How do we get past those rocks?"

"We don't." At her questioning glance, he added, "We'll be putting down anchor just outside the nearest ring of them and using the rowboat to go ashore."

Prion appeared at her elbow, the sudden nearness making her jump. He gave her a brief nod with an unreadable look, then turned to the Captain. "That our destination?"

Breck nodded and steered them closer towards it.

"Good." Prion grabbed at Leannán's arm, pulling it close. "If you don't mind, I need a brief chat with my wife before we go."

Breck nodded again, as if it meant nothing to him, and Leannán let Prion pull her across the deck to the other end of the ship.

Once they were out of earshot, Prion leaned close to her ear. "We need to talk about last night," he said. "It was... it was..."

"A onetime thing." Leannán's voice was firm, and she refused to meet his eyes. Even so, she saw his startled look in her peripheral vision and felt a flare of satisfaction. *Let him know what it feels like,* she thought.

"But—"

She turned to face him, crossing her arms across her chest. "But nothing. We need to focus on this mission. We can't let ourselves get sidetracked just because we're attracted to each other." Prion's eyes blazed at her, bright blue against his tan face. But he listened without speaking, and she gathered her courage and continued. "We are close to finding the *buidseach*. She may be on this island. But we need to keep our heads about us. Jack told me there's strange magic afoot here. Even the humans know about it. If there's any chance we can heal your sealskin, we can't mess this up."

Prion glanced over at Breck and Leannán followed his look, but Breck's back was still to them. As they watched, Jack joined the Captain and the two began to talk.

"We'll be careful," Prion growled. He took her arm and squeezed it, causing her to look back at him in surprise. "But we're not done yet," he warned. There was a dark fire in his eyes that she had trouble meeting, so she looked down at her feet. "We still have much to discuss about us."

"There is no us," she said firmly. "The faster you understand that, the faster we can get this mission taken care of."

Prion made a disgruntled noise, but let her arm go. After a moment, she risked a glance at him and saw him staring at the island, the muscles in his jaw clenching and unclenching.

He's not happy, she thought. *He's not used to being denied anything.*

Well, you certainly didn't deny him last night, a small voice in her mind spoke up. She flushed at the thought. No, she hadn't denied him anything then.

But that will be the last, she thought. No more dalliances. She refused to be a pawn for him, a way to pass the time.

"It's time," Prion said. His voice was distant, as if he were deep in thought.

She took a deep breath. "Then let's go."

CHAPTER 7

THEY DROPPED ANCHOR A few hundred yards out, then lowered the rowboat. Jack stayed behind to man the ship, while Breck rowed Prion and Leannán out. They all carried bags with them, Leannán's and Prion's both containing their sealskins and an overnight set of clothes, and Breck's containing gods only knew what. But Leannán was grateful for the company, even if it was only going to go as far as the shore.

Breck carefully navigated the rocks, steering as cleanly between them as possible. He didn't take a direct path to the island—the rocks made that impossible—but he zig-zagged his way there until they docked the boat on a sandy beach.

As the boat's bottom scraped against the sand, Breck gave them both a level look. "You should know that I'm only going to stay as long as we have daylight."

"That's fine," Leannán said with a smile. "We can stay the night with my family and meet you here tomorrow morning."

"No," Breck said. "You don't understand. These waters are dangerous come nightfall. Getting here may have seemed easy, but there's something about this area that crashes any boat that comes at night. I'll not be caught out in nothing more than a rowboat without the sun at my back. If we aren't done by the time night falls, you're on your own."

They stared at him in shocked horror. Only the daylight to find the *buidseach* and fix the sealskin? They didn't even know where on the island she was!

"You can't do that," Prion cried. "We need more time."

But Breck shook his head. "Come sundown, I'm gone and hopefully you'll be with me. Now let's get out. We're wasting the daylight."

Leannán and Prion stepped out of the boat, and Prion helped Breck haul the boat up the beach so that the waves wouldn't wash it back out to sea. While the men worked, Leannán examined their options.

The island seemed to be a single mountain peak, with a small ring of scraggly dead trees surrounding the base. She walked up to one tree. The bark was blackened and ashy, as if there had been a fire. But when she peeled back one of the flaky layers of bark, the tree was healthy and green underneath. She looked around. All the trees looked the same. Beyond them, a ring of dead thorn bushes with wickedly curved spines circled the base of the mountain as far as she could see in either direction.

Bewitched? she wondered. Perhaps made to look inhospitable so that nobody would come?

This place certainly doesn't appear warm and inviting, she thought. *It looks as though it's been winter-ravaged and burned at the same time.* She glanced through the sparse trees to the base of the mountain and saw a small opening in the thorny underbrush.

Leaving the men grunting with effort behind her, she edged closer and saw a small path leading down through the undergrowth. In fact, if she looked carefully, wasn't that a small path winding its way up the mountain, looking just on the edge of the cliff face?

With a thrill of excitement, she realized it was. She had found a way up.

"Guys, over here!" she called. When the men joined her, she pointed out what she saw. "Do we take it?"

"We don't have much choice," Prion grumbled, casting a doubtful glance up the mountain. He turned to Breck. "You'll stay with the boat."

"The hell I will!" Breck replied, putting his hands on his hips. "I've not come this far to this rotted place just to wait by the damn boat while you two go traipsing up a mountain to gods know where. For all my luck, you'll fall down the cliff and I'll lose the other half of my deposit."

He gave them a stern look, and Leannán realized, with a sinking feeling, he wasn't to be deterred. She gave a helpless look at Prion, who glared back at him.

"You have no idea what kind of danger this place has," Prion warned.

"I think I have a might better idea than you do," Breck countered. "I know the stories. And I'll be damned if I let some *buidseach* run me off." Leannán and Prion exchanged startled glances, then stared at Breck. "What?" he said, looking back and forth between their startled faces. "I heard you on the deck this morning. Sound carries on the water, you know. And I don't know why you two are trying to fix a sealskin, though I have my own hunch." He nodded at them gravely. "I know the stories."

Leannán felt a flush creep up her neck and warm her cheeks. He knew?

"But I'm not letting you two go alone." Breck fished in his pocket and drew out a small knife in a leather sheath. "If anything goes sideways, I've got this, which is a sight more than you two seem to have."

"This isn't a job for knives," Prion said. "This is a matter of mag—"

"Delicacy," Leannán broke in. She didn't know how much the human suspected, but she knew it was better to leave some things to his imagination rather than confirm them. "This is a matter of great delicacy. My family—" Breck gave a derisive snort as if to say she wasn't fooling him. "*My family*," she continued through gritted teeth, "may not be accustomed to visitors. It's best if we go alone."

But Breck turned a stony glare on her and simply waited.

After several moments, Prion sighed and turned to Leannán. "Look, he'll probably just follow us, anyway. Might as well take him. We're not even sure what we're getting into."

Leannán growled in frustration. Was nothing going to go right on this trip? "Fine. But you let us do the talking! And whatever you hear, you must never repeat. There is strange magic here, and you don't know what you're meddling with." The empty threat scared her as much as it seemed to scare Breck, because he gave a nervous glance up the mountain, then turned to her and nodded once in acknowledgment.

With one last look out at the *Tamed Tempest*, which looked like a small toy ship in the distance, she turned and followed Prion to the entrance to the path with Breck bringing up the rear.

The path was steep, and it didn't take long for Prion to become winded and slow.

Leannán glanced behind her and saw Breck several feet back. "Everything okay?" Leannán asked Prion quietly.

He glared at her, but she sensed his anger wasn't directed at her but at himself. "Fine. I'm just getting so tired so quickly... My human form isn't used to working this hard."

"This is hardly the one-and-done sort of situation you're used to experiencing as a human," she said dryly. He pursed his lips but didn't disagree.

They pushed on.

They seemed to have only been walking for an hour, but Leannán noticed the sun had moved several inches lower towards the horizon.

Come sundown, I'm gone and hopefully you'll be with me, Breck had said. He hadn't mentioned the passing of time again, but she couldn't shake the nagging feeling that they were moving too slowly, that the daylight was creeping faster than it should have been. Hadn't it only been late morning when they'd arrived at the island? And now here the day was close to two-thirds gone.

She remembered what Jack had told her about strange magic.

Well, something was certainly going wrong.

The trail leveled off and twisted downward, which enabled Prion to pick up the pace somewhat. But moments later, he halted, and Leannán bumped into him.

"What is it?" she asked, peering around him.

The path led into a large cave opening. From where they stood, they could hear the rush of falling water. A strange light seemed to emanate from the cave, though they couldn't tell what the light source was.

"Now what?" Prion asked her. He seemed hesitant to enter.

"We go in," Breck answered from behind them. "Unless you want to head back now and forget the whole thing?"

Prion and Leannán exchanged an uncertain glance, then she nodded her head towards the cave. As Prion stepped forward, she felt him slip his hand in hers and she squeezed it gratefully.

They entered the cave and noticed a tall waterfall falling down the rock wall into a large pool of water. The light source seemed to come from underwater somehow. They looked around the cave, but there were no entrances or exits other than the one they came through.

"What do we do now?" Prion asked. "It's a dead end."

Leannán glanced behind them and saw with a sinking sensation in the pit of her stomach that the light outside was dimmer than before. Dusk was falling.

"We don't have time to wait," she said and bent to one knee. She shrugged off her bag and pulled out her sealskin.

Prion grabbed her shoulder and gave a quick glance at Breck, who was looking on with curiosity. "No, Leannán, you can't. Not here."

"We don't have any choice, Prion. We can't turn back, and we can't go forward without going underwater. I need to see how long we have to be underwater. It's a deathtrap to try going in there without knowing how long we have to go. And we're running out of time."

"You don't plan on diving in there by yourself, do you?" Breck asked in a surprised voice, as she began shucking out of her clothing. "Let me go."

But Leannán was already done. As soon as her clothes hit the rocky floor, she pulled her sealskin over her shoulders and jumped into the water. Once submerged, she fastened the hooks at her belly and curled into the change.

Pain and pleasure all at once. The feeling of pulling on a favorite piece of clothing, an old familiar sense of coming home. Of her arms shortening, becoming stronger, more flexible. Her legs coming together into one strong set of flippers. Her body feeling lighter and more buoyant as she came into her element. Then she was in her seal form entirely.

She bobbed back to the surface and barked once at them. Before she dove under, she registered Breck's shocked face, feeling a ripple of unease. They were never to change in front of a human. She hoped it wouldn't come back to bite them both later.

For a moment, she paused, savoring the sight of the murky water coming into clear focus as her seal eyes adapted to the dim water view. She glanced around the pool, noting the surprising depth. But she didn't have time to explore; she followed the light.

The light led her through an underwater tunnel and she shot down it, noting the smaller pathways that branched off to either side and ignoring them. She kept to where the light was brightest, letting it grow lighter as she swam. She counted her pulse in her head, trying to imagine Prion's human lungs and how long they could last without fresh air.

... 5 heartbeats, 6 heartbeats, 7 heartbeats, 8...

At 50 heartbeats, the light flared brightest, and she saw an opening in the tunnel above just wide enough for her body. She poked her head out, wary of predators, but saw only another empty cave. The light source, she saw, were hundreds of candles burning throughout the cave.

Certain she was alone, she heaved her bulky body out of the opening and onto the cave floor. Glancing around, she saw the candles were in small crevices lining the walls, fused in place by clumps of melted wax. The candles were different colors—purple, pink, black, white—making the cave appear covered in a patchwork quilt of light.

She looked around for an exit, another waterway tunnel, an opening in the wall... and saw nothing. The floor was smooth, save for her exit hole, and the only break in the wall of candles was a small curved patch that looked as if it had a chalk outline scraped in the rough shape of a door. Strange streaks ran down the wall from a central point, and above it were selkie runes inscribed in a message: "Welcome, sister."

But the wall was smooth, unlined with candles, and firm when she lumbered over and pressed a flipper against it.

They were out of luck.

The cave was another dead end.

CHAPTER 8

"So now what?" Prion asked. He took in the cave, trying to ignore the alluring image of Leannán sitting naked on the edge of the pool in the cave with her sopping sealskin balled in her lap. He and Breck had insisted on following her to the second cave to see for themselves.

Prion hadn't been sure he could handle the swim with his human lung power, but he'd made it with her swimming beside him, ready to change and give him a breath underwater if she had to.

But he hadn't needed it. He'd emerged gasping, but unharmed at the other end. Breck had handled the swim better, as if he were used to being submerged for long periods. It hadn't been a surprise to Prion.

But they obviously were to him.

The second Breck emerged from the hole, he pointed an accusing finger at Leannán. "You're a witch!"

"Not a witch," she corrected. "A selkie. We can—"

"Change into human form from a seal, yeah, I know," he grumbled. "I know the lore. But it might as well be witchcraft."

She shrugged, as if she'd been called worse before, though never by a human. "It's not exactly something I can help. It's just the way I was born."

"And are you one, too?" Breck asked Prion.

Prion just glowered at him, which was all the answer he needed. Breck snorted and passed a hand through his hair. "Saints alive, I never thought I'd live to see the day."

"How about you help us figure out how to handle this situation?" Prion snapped.

"How about first she put on some clothes?" Breck retorted. "I'm not wandering around this island with a naked selkie."

Prion glared at him, but Leannán began pulling on her wet clothes. She lifted her spare set of clothes out of her bag so she could stow her sealskin away, and grimaced as they dripped water onto the floor. "It seemed a good idea at the time..."

While she fiddled with her bag, Prion felt a sudden overwhelming sense of dread. What were they walking into? What kind of magic could this *buidseach* wield? It could all go wrong so fast...

He shook his head. That kind of thinking wasn't productive. He steeled himself. This would work. It had to. And yet... he looked at Leannán. She had no idea what she was getting into, either with this situation or with him. She had asked for nothing and had gotten close to nothing in return.

He thought of that amazing night they shared. It had rocked him, to be sure, but it had also changed how he felt in an irreparable way. There was a tie between them, a bond that hadn't been there before, and now it felt like something tangible stretching between them. But how was he to show it to her? He gave Breck a surreptitious glance. The human was just in the way. He could hardly declare himself now, of all times.

Then he had an idea.

He plucked the necklace from around his neck and held it up. His grandsire's ring hung in the air, sparkling in the candlelight. "Leannán?" he said hesitantly. She looked up at him with a question on her face. He held out his hand to her. Frowning, she placed her hand in his, and he felt a thrill of excitement at the realization that she hadn't even hesitated. Such trust in him. He didn't deserve it.

"I want you to have this," he told her, and slipped the ring's cord over her head.

She held the ring up to her face and examined it. "Prion, your grandsire's ring? I can't take this?" She reached up to remove the necklace, but he shook his head and pressed her hands over her own chest. Her skin was warm beneath his and he felt a tingle run through him, similar to the magic that had once bound him to his sealskin.

"If something goes wrong here, anything at all, and we get separated, take this to my mother. She'll know you didn't just abandon me."

"I would never—" Leannán started, but he held up a hand.

"Just promise me you'll wear it?"

She looked back down at it again, then nodded. She leaned forward, as if waiting for his kiss, and he bent to claim it.

Breck cleared his throat. "If we're done with the mushy stuff? We have a problem to solve."

Prion straightened, glaring at him, then glanced over at the chalk outline of the doorway. Breck had a point, as annoying as his timing was. He walked over to it and pressed his hand in the area above the strange brown streaks. "It looks like blood," he said. "But... from what?"

"From the entrants," Breck said. When they both turned to look at him, he shrugged. "It's common knowledge. Magic pays a price. I'll bet the price to enter is blood magic." When they continued to stare, he rolled his eyes and got to his feet. He pulled his knife from his pocket and sliced a small cut along the meaty edge of his palm. Then he walked over to the door and placed his hand against the smooth rock wall above the brown streaks.

The chalk outline of the doorway flared to life and shimmered, sending a shower of sparks into the air.

Prion felt a rush of excitement. *It's working!* he thought.

Then the shimmer faded and disappeared. The chalk outline, though still there, looked... different, somehow, in a way she couldn't put his finger on.

They all stared around them, waiting. But the candles continued to flicker like they had been, and nothing else happened.

"Let me try," Prion said. He took Breck's knife and cut the same wound along his palm, then pressed his hand to the wall over Breck's bloody hand print. The outline flared to life again, sending up sparks. Then, after a few heartbeats, it faded away again as if it had never happened.

"Look, the outline," Breck said, pointing. "It's faded."

As he said it, that's what Prion realized had looked different. The chalk outline was less distinct than it had been before, and even less so now that Prion had pressed his hand to the wall. It was barely visible in the dim light, and he wondered what would happen if the outline disappeared all together.

"What happens when it's gone?" Breck asked in a hushed tone, echoing his thoughts.

"We're stuck," Leannán said in a flat voice. "There's no way through."

Prion's mind raced. There had to be a way through. All signs pointed towards it being the only way forward. This had to be the way! He examined the cave again, taking in the candles, the long-standing layers of melted wax. Someone had to come refresh those candles when they went out. Someone had to access this area.

He looked back at the doorway, at the chalk outline and the bloody streaks and the message in runes saying, *"Welcome, sister."*

Welcome, sister.

"Maybe," he said, testing the words as he said them, "it takes a woman to do it."

"That's ridiculous," Breck scoffed.

Prion pointed towards the runes and told him what they meant. "Magic has a price, but doesn't it also have rules? I think it means only a female can do it."

Prion and Breck exchanged dubious glances, then looked at Leannán.

"We don't have much of a choice," Prion urged. He could feel time ticking down behind him and hoped night hadn't already fallen.

Finally, the men both nodded, and Breck handed over the knife, hilt-first.

Leannán took it with a grimace, obviously hating the feel of the bone hilt in her hands. She gave a quick slash at her palm, nicking the fleshy part below her thumb, and walked over to press her hand against the wall, over the fresh hand prints.

The sparks flew as the outline flared to life. Only this time, instead of dying out, the cave began to rumble. Prion rushed forward to grip her shoulder, bending over her to protect her, and squeezed his eyes shut.

After several long moments, the quaking subsided.

"Prion," Leannán said in an awestruck voice. "Look."

Prion opened his eyes to see the chalk outline was gone, replaced by a deep groove cut into the stone. Beneath Leannán's hand, a small outcropping had appeared, like a handle.

She applied tentative pressure to it, and the door swung open.

The three of them exchanged nervous glances, then pushed it all the way so they could enter. Inside was a long stone hallway, lit with torches on either side. But when Prion looked closer at them, he noticed that although there was wood and pitch on them, no smoke emitted from the flames.

"Bewitched," Breck grumbled. "More selkie magic?"

Leannán and Prion shrugged in unison. "Your guess is as good as mine."

Leannán started down the hallway, but Breck put a restraining hand on her shoulder. Prion quickly pulled it off, and the two men stared at each other in sudden animosity.

"You'll keep your hands to yourself," Prion growled, his eyes blazing. How dare this human attempt to put hands on his woman?

Breck glared at him, but when he spoke, it was to Leannán. "I think it's time you explain to me what's going on here. Why are we here? And what should we expect to find at the end of that hallway?"

Prion's face contorted into a snarl as he opened his mouth, but Leannán put a hand on his chest. "It's fine. He deserves to know. He's come this far with us." She gave Breck a brief explanation of the attack on Prion's skin and their search for the *buidseach*.

"And you think she's here," Breck said. It wasn't a question.

Leannán nodded. "We hope so. And if we're right, she'll repair Prion's skin so that he can change again. But we have to hurry—we don't know what kind of magic happens at nightfall."

"I don't intend to be here to find out," Breck agreed. "But I'm too curious to leave. Let's get going."

Prion noticed Breck's knife was out and that he'd shifted it to his uninjured hand. It was a smart move, and he wished he'd brought some kind of weapon, too. It would feel good to have something in his hand.

In a flash of inspiration, he reached up and took down a torch. Its heft felt solid in his hand, comforting. "Okay," he said. "Let's go."

They walked down the hallway slowly, mindful of the time passing, but hesitant to encounter any surprises. After a few moments, the gloom parted, and they saw a door at the other end.

They stepped up to it and halted.

"Now what?" Prion whispered.

Leannán gulped. "I suppose we knock."

Prion raised his fist, but Leannán pushed it back down. "Remember the cave? *Welcome, sister*? I think I'm supposed to do it."

"Then get on with it," Breck growled from behind them.

Prion shot him a look of intense dislike as Leannán raised her hand and knocked three times.

For a long moment, there was nothing. Then there was the click of a door latch disengaging, and the door cracked open.

Leannán took a deep breath and pushed it the rest of the way, remaining on the threshold. Prion stepped in front of her, instinctively protective, and thrust the torch in front of him. Behind them, Prion heard a rustle as Breck raised his knife at the ready.

"I didn't expect three of you," a low, melodic voice said. "Interesting."

Prion held the torch to one side, so the light did not blind him, and gave his eyes a moment to adjust. Inside the room, a woman stood, dressed in simple gray robes. Her long gray hair cascaded down either side of her shoulders like a shroud, all the way down to her hips. Her feet were bare.

Around her neck, several necklaces held bone and stone talismans. Prion recognized a hag stone, a small black stone with a natural hole in the middle, known for protection and healing. He also saw a small, curved talon, like that of a bird of prey. The rest were lost in the jumble of items strewn on a cord.

"Who are you?" she asked.

"We could ask you the same question," Breck retorted. He'd moved to stand next to Leannán. Prion set his shoulder slightly in front of Breck's, to give the human the understanding that he wasn't in charge here. He crossed his arms over his chest and gave a quick glower at Breck, who pursed his lips and glared back.

"Yes, but you're in *my* home," the woman responded with a small smile. But Prion noticed her eyes were very sharp, and the smile didn't reach them. "Common courtesy demands you greet me first."

"Courtesy be dam—" Breck began, but Leannán cut him off.

"We are here to seek your help."

"My help?" the woman laughed with a disdainful toss of her head. "You've come a long way for nothing, then. I don't help humans."

"The human doesn't request your help," Leannán said in a firm voice. "Your Prince does."

"He's not *my* Prince," the woman said. "He's yours. I am of no clan. Therefore, I'm not bound to help him, as you are. Though you're bound in a different way, perhaps?" Her voice turned sly. "I think bonds of affection have more to do with your help than your sense of duty. Tell me, does he know your secret, girl? Does he know your plans once this mission is over?"

Prion gave Leannán a sharp glance. What was this woman talking about? What plans could Leannán have other than to return to their clan together?

"Look," Prion said in a soothing voice. "I think we've gotten off wrong. Let's restart, shall we?" He put his hand on his chest, calling on all the diplomacy his parents had forced him to learn for their cross-clan relations. "I am requesting your help. Your assistance would prove most valuable, and would put my clan in your debt. We are a formidable group, and—"

"And what you want is impossible," the woman said.

Prion felt the floor drop from underneath him.

CHAPTER 9

"WHAT'S YOUR NAME?" LEANNÁN asked, with a nervous glance at Prion. His expression had turned stoney, and she knew his temper was close to the surface. If she could smooth this situation, she would. She called on all her skills as a handmaiden, one trained to see through problems to find their solutions.

"There's power in names," the woman replied with a calculated glance up and down Leannán's slight form. "Why should I tell you?"

"Because your life depends on it," Prion growled.

Leannán put a hand on his forearm, and he flashed her a sullen glance before planting his free hand on his hip. "Because we need your help," she said softly. "We aren't here to harm you."

The woman snorted in derision and looked pointedly away.

"I'm Leannán, and this is Prion."

The woman's eyes flicked to Prion. "Prince Prion? Of Liath Clann?" she asked.

Prion glanced at Leannán, then nodded. "You've heard of me?"

"Your reputation precedes you, my lord," the woman said. "You were in the court of the Great Elder as a child." Prion nodded, and the woman nodded as if this confirmed something she'd already suspected. "You saved his life."

Prion's eyes burned in his face as he stared at her with a hungry expression, as if he knew he was close to what he sought. "Did we know each other there?"

"No, but I heard about you. Few have a selkie like that in their debt."

"I would call in that debt a hundred times over if I thought he could help me now."

"My name is Harper," the woman said, "and what do you need help with?" Though she hadn't moved, her bearing was one of a regal queen speaking to her subjects.

Without breaking eye contact with her, Prion held out his hand. Leannán passed him the bag containing his torn sealskin and took the torch from him. Prion's expression was stark as he pulled out the skin, handling it with the utmost care, then held out at arm's length. It unfurled like a ruined tapestry, the rips in the blubber pushing through like gray ropes in the fur.

Without speaking, Harper eyed the sealskin. Then she looked at Prion. "And what is it you wish of me?"

"I was told you could fix this damage," he said in an incredulous voice, as if astounded she hadn't gleaned his intent already.

"Nobody can heal a skin that has been wrought so badly."

Prion stared at her, still holding out his pelt as if she needed more time to decide. "You only looked at it for a few seconds," he said. "Maybe if you touch it—" He stepped forward into the room.

"I will not," she said, recoiling slightly, showing emotion for the first time as fear rippled across her face. "I would not dare touch something that has been so befouled."

Prion's expression darkened, and he lowered the pelt so that his arms hung at his sides.

Leannán gave him an anxious glance. She cleared her throat. "Perhaps if you looked closer at it—"

"No," Prion interrupted. His eyes stayed on Harper as he spoke. "She said she wouldn't do it." He bent and began stuffing his sealskin back in his bag with angry, jerky motions.

"If she can't, we'll find someone who can," Leannán began, but Prion held up a hand to cut her off as he straightened.

"She didn't say she *couldn't*." His voice was soft, but his eyes were hard as gems in his face.

For several long moments, Harper and Prion stared at each other. Harper looked composed, while Prion's features were as immobile as stone. Then Prion turned to Breck. "Take hold of her."

Breck cast an incredulous glance back and forth between Prion and Harper. "You want me to do what now?" His eyebrows had disappeared into his hairline.

"I said—" Prion barked, but was startled by a voice from behind him.

"I'll take care of that," a loud voice boomed.

They whirled to see a man behind them holding a sword at their backs. Flanking him were three more men, all holding swords at the ready. One man towered over the others by at least a head, while the other two appeared to be identical twins.

"What is the meaning of this?" a voice barked. They all turned to look in Harper's direction, but instead, there was a strange man standing where she had been. He was the same height as Harper, but his hair was cut short to his head. He had a long beard and mustache that obscured his mouth. Though he was dressed in a simple brown tunic, around his neck were the same necklaces Harper wore. The man pointed towards the door. "Leave here now or—"

"Or else what?" the man sneered. He took two steps forward, coming into the light of Leannán's torch.

"Adair!" Breck hissed. "You backstabbing snake! What the hell do you think you're doing here?"

"Following you to a treasure, obviously." Adair shrugged with one shoulder. He tossed his hair out of his eyes and grinned at them. "But you took me on a chase. When I heard you were headed to Little Kill Island, I knew there had to be something more going on. And it appears I was right..." He gestured with his sword tip at the strange man. "You, witch woman. What manner of magic do you deal in?"

"I'm no witch woman," the man said in surprise. He put a hand on his chest. "I'm just a simple hermit. I go by Amadán."

"Sure," Adair sneered, with a pointed look around the room. He stepped forward and used his sword tip to lift the layers of necklaces around Amadán's neck and cocked an eyebrow at him. "Too bad I heard everything you said to them."

Amadán sneered at him, then shook his head in a motion that began with his head and increased so that his whole body was shaking from side-to-side. The glamour fell away like water pouring down a rock face, and Harper stood there, glaring at Adair.

"I deal in whatever interests me," Harper said in a casual tone, as if not staring down a handful of men who could kill her three times over. "What sort of magic are you interested in?"

"Power." Adair hissed the word with a breathy eagerness. "I want more power than anyone else on the island. I want to be in charge. How do I make that happen?"

Prion looked over his shoulder, risking a glance at the *buidseach*. Did Adair know who he was speaking to? He assumed not, given that he was handling the interaction so casually. But perhaps that was his ego talking instead of his reason. The short impression he had of the man certainly indicated it could be that way.

Harper put a finger to her chin, eyeing Adair with a calculating look. Then she began to bustle around the small room, gathering small components into a small pouch. Prion waited tensely, hoping there would be a break where he could buy Leannán some time to run. He wondered how he would indicate his plan to her, though. Perhaps if he could get close enough to whisper in her ear? He stepped to one side, feigning casualty, and leaned towards Leannán.

"Uh-uh," one of Adair's men said, with a twitch of his sword. "Stay still."

Prion smoldered at him, letting all his fury leek into his expression. The man swallowed hard and took an involuntary step back, but his sword didn't waver.

Harper stepped past him and walked up to Adair. She held out the small pouch. "Steep this in hot water when you return home. Then eat the remains in the bottom of the cup, and say this..." She leaned forward and whispered in his ear. As she spoke, Adair's eyes gleamed and his smile widened.

When she straightened, he looked down at her. "And that will give me power?" She nodded serenely. "Then I thank you, witch woman." He sheathed his sword and began to stroll around the room. He rifled through the papers on the small wooden desk in the corner and fiddled with a trio of glass bottles on a shelf. They were filled with various colors of liquid and small items that looked to Prion like finger bones.

"I wouldn't touch that!" Harper warned. "Very potent stuff."

Adair gave her a crooked smile and put his hands in the air in mock surrender. But the smile never left his face as he wandered the room, plucking at this treasure and that, and examining the pictures carved into the stone walls.

He stopped at a chiseled carving of a seal arcing through the air, with swirls of glittering clouds around it. The stone was carved in such a way that the clouds sparkled like diamonds in the light, giving the appearance of water spray. Below the carving was a small wooden box.

He fingered the lid.

"Leave that!" Harper called. "That is a very dangerous tool. Touching that will bring serious pain down upon you."

The smile slipped from his face as Adair turned to peer at her. He gave her an appraising glance, looked back down at the box, then looked back at Harper. Even Prion could see the tension radiating from her shoulders as she watched him.

Then Adair gave a small smile and lifted the lid. He frowned down at the contents, then reached in and pulled out a long, grey pelt.

"What's this?" he mused. "A wolfskin? Here?" He rolled it in hands, letting the silky mass ripple and gleam in the light. He brought it closer to Leannán's torch and held it up. Prion saw with horror the small fasteners lining one side of the skin.

Not a wolfskin. A sealskin.

Her sealskin.

Prion gave her a sharp glance, noting the frozen look on her face, then looked back at Adair. Did he realize what he was holding? Did he realize the power he held in his hands? To hold a selkie's sealskin was to control the selkie, to enslave them until they could gain possession of it again. What could Adair do with a *buidseach* at his beck and call?

Adair lowered the skin, looking disappointed. Prion breathed a quiet sigh of relief.

Then Adair looked at his companions. "Bring them. All of them."

"Even the witch?" one of the twins asked with a nervous glance at Harper.

"Especially the witch," Adair replied, then turned and began walking out of the room, the sealskin clutched in his hands.

"You can't do this!" Harper cried, finally showing something other than serene composure. "I gave you what you want! Let me go. There is magic here, magic even beyond my control. Magical safeguards that took a long time to put in place—I can't call them off so easily! Give me back my things and I can—"

Adair whirled and lunged forward so that they were in kissing distance. His eyes blazed like beacons from his flushed face. "You can what?" His voice was deceptively soft. "Let you go and you'll... give me my every desire?" He laughed, tossing his head back in a bellow of laughter. "My dear, you already will. You just don't know it yet." He gave her a winsome smile, while she stared at him, then turned and walked down the hall. "Move out, men!"

Her eyes blazing, she turned to face the man nearest her who held a sword. "You wouldn't dare," she hissed. "Touch me and you'll be—"

Quick as a snake, the man moved, slamming the hilt of the sword into her face at the temple. Her eyes rolled back in her head, and she slumped forward. The man bent and caught her, slinging her smoothly over his shoulder. Her arms dangled in the waterfall of her hair as the man turned and carried her out of the room.

Prion felt his chance slipping away. He lunged towards the twin closest to him, intending to slam the man into the wall and seize his sword, but the tall man pulled Leannán close. His sword raised to her throat, and the man gave him a lopsided smile. "I don't think you want to do that," the man said soothingly, as if talking to a feral animal. "Just move along and there'll be no trouble."

"Where are you taking us?" Leannán ground out.

"Back to the ship," the tall man said, lowering his sword and pushing her in front of him so hard she stumbled. "Then you and your friends will be let go. The Captain's got what he came for."

Prion caught Leannán by the shoulders and steadied her. "When we're in the water, shift and get away," he whispered into her ear.

But she shook her head. "We're on our honeymoon," she said loudly, raising her voice so the other men could hear, though she pretended to be talking to him. "We just wanted a baby. There's nothing wrong with seeking help from a witch woman. Captain Adair will see that, surely."

The men all laughed as they gestured for Prion and Leannán to precede them out of the room.

"Want help with a baby?" one of the twins leered. "We can help with that..."

Prion turned a furious glare on him, and both twins jeered.

"Don't take Bryce so seriously, lad," the tall man laughed, jerking his chin at the twin who'd spoken. "The Captain's a man of his word." He pointed at the other twin with his sword. "Brodie, get that captain up here."

"Tell that to Harper," Breck muttered as Brodie hustled him past them.

"Well, the Captain didn't promise *her* nothing, now did he?" jeered Bryce. Prion seethed, vowing to remember all of them, every detail. If anything happened to Leannán, he would hunt them down.

Brodie slapped his twin's shoulder and laughed.

But Prion realized Adair hadn't promised them anything, either.

CHAPTER 10

BY THE TIME ADAIR'S men emerged with them on the mountain path, the sun had just set over the horizon. They had lashed Harper's unconscious body to Bryce's back with a length of rope they pulled from Breck's bag.

"Aren't you worried she'll drown?" Prion demanded as they lowered her body into the hole in the candlelit cave.

Adair, standing to one side, frowned with negligent grace. "Not particularly. If she drowns, she drowns. But I'm counting on her magic to save her." He gave Prion a cocky grin. "We'll see what kind of witch she really is, I guess."

Prion clenched his jaws to keep back the angry retort that threatened to burst from his lips. *Keep calm,* he told himself. *Stay collected. We might get out of this yet.*

They swam back through the underwater tunnel, and Prion was relieved to see that Harper was still breathing when they emerged on the other side. As long as she was alive, there was a chance his sealskin could be repaired. Thankfully, Adair's men had only done cursory investigations into his or Leannán's packs—they'd seen the spare set of clothes wrapped around the sealskins and had looked no deeper.

Adair's men bound their hands behind their backs with cut lengths of Breck's rope. "For insurance, mind," the tall man said in a reassuring voice. His manner was one of doing a household chore that's tedious but not unpleasant. He even hummed while he did it.

They were halfway down the trail leading down the mountain when the wind picked up. A howling started from the far side of the mountain, loud enough that Adair's men stopped to look around, their swords raised.

Prion stepped closer to Leannán and put her body between him and the mountain wall.

"Behind us!" one of the twins screamed, and they all whirled to look.

A giant red bull was charging through the air towards them, curving around the mountain stone as if it had started on the same path as them just further up. It was made of gas and vapor that flickered like flames, and when it snorted, actual fire shot in twin balls into the air above their heads.

They all broke into a run, captive and captor roles forgotten in their terror as they slipped and skidded on the gravel path.

The bull bellowed as it charged past them, overshooting them. It curved in the air, rolling back on its haunches to whirl back towards them, bellowing and screaming like a banshee from the seventh level of hell.

"Run!" Prion screamed at Leannán, planting a hand on her shoulder and pushing her forward. "Don't stop!" Ahead of them, Breck raced past the twins and overtook the tall man, whose long legs loped down the path like a deer.

They all bolted down the path, dodging fireballs shooting from the bull's nostrils that crashed into explosive firebombs behind them. Prion risked a glance over his shoulder. To his horror, he saw the bull pause and inhale, its barrel-like sides heaving open like bellows. Two small fireballs appeared in its nostrils, and Prion knew, in the pit of his stomach, they wouldn't be fast enough.

He shoved Leannán to one side at the last minute, almost sending her off the path cliff into the singed brush beyond as he heard the roar behind him, in his ears, and in his head. He twisted away, keeping one hand planted on her shoulder, the only thing holding her on the path, as the heat exploded into the rock wall behind him.

Fire ate at his thigh, and he screamed, letting go of Leannán long enough to bat furiously at his pants leg, where small flames licked and tore at his wet clothing. The fire went out, even as a searing burn echoed where it had eaten through the fabric to his skin beneath. But still he kept running, limping as fast as he could on his injured leg, keeping between Leannán and the bull as best as he could.

When the three boats came into sight on the beach, Prion glanced again over his shoulder to see the bull fall back a step as it inhaled again, readying another fireball blast. Gritting his teeth, he put his head down and tore after Leannán, knowing the next shot could consume them both.

As they reached the boats, Adair in the lead, Prion saw Bryce pitch Harper's unconscious body into one and heave his own shoulder into the prow of the boat to push it into the water.

As Bryce leapt into the boat and began rowing, Prion saw Adair grabbed a fistful of Breck's clothes at the shoulder as Breck tried to jump into his own boat.

"Not that one!" he snarled, as he shoved Breck towards his own rowboat.

Breck half-fell into Adair's boat as Adair put his shoulder into the front and began to shove it into the water. Brodie piled in after him.

The tall man slowed and planted his feet in the sand, turning so that he could snag Leannán by the upper arm.

"Hey!" Prion shouted, trying to wrestle the man's grip from her arm, but as he did so the bull bellowed from behind him again, and he decided living was the better option. He grabbed Leannán's other hand and pulled her into the remaining empty boat, the one Breck and them had sailed in on. The tall man let go long enough to shove the boat into the water and clamber in as Breck began rowing away, Adair's sword at his neck.

The tall man picked up the oars and began heaving to get them away from the island. Over his shoulder, Prion watched as the bull reached the beach. It galloped onto the sand, then splashed into the ocean with its front legs. As its body hit the water, a red mist rose, and the bull gave a mighty bellow that made Prion and Leannán clap their hands over their ears while the tall man rowed harder.

The darkness rose around them as they headed away from the beach, with the water more turbulent than Prion remembered it being as the bull grew smaller and smaller behind them.

He considered tossing Leannán and her bag overboard, knowing she'd get away safely. But there was Harper to worry about. If he gave them away now, there was no chance of him ever getting her to heal his sealskin. Better to go with Leannán's plan of pretending they were honeymooners trying to get help conceiving. It was a fast story she'd come up with in the moment, but it was solid. He was proud of her for her fast thinking.

If we make it through this, he thought, *I'm going to tell her how clever she was.*

Though, if he were being honest with himself, there were other things he was going to have to tell her, too. Like the fact that in the heat of the moment, when the bull was raging behind them, his only thought had been for her safety and not his own. Even now, as the bellows of the bull faded into the sound of the surf around them, his stomach still clenched with terror at the thought that she might have been hurt. For her to be hurt was so much worse than if he had been.

He paused, ignoring the grunts of the tall man as he navigated them carefully around the first half-submerged rock. He couldn't remember the last time he'd cared for someone more than himself, had put their needs first, and it was like a breath of fresh sea air to realize that his feelings for her had changed.

But that's if we make it out of this mess, he promised himself. No, not if, *when.* When they made it out of this, he was going to tell her how he felt, these new feelings that were emerging inside him. He just had to find the right time.

CHAPTER II

BACK ON ADAIR'S SHIP, *The Hellion*, the tension was as thick as the salty air. Bryce had disappeared below-deck with a still-unconscious Harper, while the tall man and Brodie had ushered Prion, Leannán, and Breck to the top deck, where Adair appraised them.

"Now what to do with you?" he mused, fingering his chin. He pointed to Leannán, who gulped.

I am the handmaiden to the selkie Queen, she told herself. *I can handle more than this human.* She straightened her shoulders, and from the corner of her eye, saw Prion nod in approval.

"What is your business with the witch woman?" Adair asked. "Why did you travel so far to find her?"

"They're trying to have a baby, Captain," Brodie spoke up, then hunched as Adair gave him a withering glance.

"I wanted to hear it from her lips," Adair snarled. Then he looked pointedly at Leannán and waited.

"There's not much else to it," she admitted, trying to sound uncertain and scared. If Adair thought them to be a desperate couple, maybe he would let them go quickly. "We want to have a child and have had little luck." She blushed and looked down at her hands. "We had heard of a witch woman who had helped others do such things. We heard it was possible—"

"Where did you hear about her?" Adair asked.

"What?" Leannán's head rose to meet his eyes in genuine confusion.

"Where did you hear about her?" Adair repeated. "Where are you from?"

She shot a panicked look at Prion, who limped forward. "From Lochton," he said quickly. "Off the southern coast."

"Pretty far from the southern coast," Adair said in a smooth voice.

"We are desperate, sir," Leannán said. She gave him an entreating look. "Look, do with her what you will, but let us talk to her first. Please let her help us before you take her away."

"How do you suppose she can help you, given her current situation?"

"I don't know... with a potion? A spell? I don't know how these things work any more than I know how the first spark of life begins. But we've tried for so long and—"

"She can't help you now," he said in a final tone. "Best that you forget her and go about your lives."

Leannán tried to work up tears, but then thought better of it. Best not to overplay the act. She looked at Prion sadly, then nodded as if accepting her fate. Prion put an arm around her shoulders, and they stood together with bowed heads.

After a moment, Leannán risked a peek at Adair. He looked bored and was examining the sealskin in his hands, petting the glossy topcoat and then turning it over to see the shiny layer of blubber underneath. "Take them away," he said with a negligent wave of his hand. He seemed too absorbed in the skin to care what happened to them.

The tall man stowed Breck, Leannán, and Prion in the cargo hold, thankfully after unbinding their hands. Brodie followed and tossed their bags in the corner along with some bandages.

"For the leg," he grunted, jerking his chin at Prion.

"Not worried we'll try to swim away, are you?" Breck spat at the tall man while rubbing his wrists.

But the man just smiled serenely and shook his head. "Not with what's running in these waters, no. You wouldn't get very far."

Leannán shot an anxious look at Prion, but he was watching Breck with a small smile on his face.

Once Adair's men had left the hold, Breck turned to them. "I think we've pulled one over. He's too interested in that witch woman to care about us. He thinks he's won."

"So, what will he do now?" Leannán asked, bending to retrieve the bandages Brodie had chucked into the corner. She pulled a long strip free and knelt to wind it around Prion's injured thigh, wincing at the angry red burn skin that peeked out through his ripped pants.

"Probably return us to my ship."

"But what about Harper?" Leannán blurted out.

"What about her?" Prion said, rounding on her. "That *buidseach* got what she deserved." He spat the term with as much disgust as he could muster.

She stared up at him, shocked. "But she didn't do anything to—"

"That's right," Prion growled, glaring down at her. "She didn't do anything. I say let her to her own fate."

"I'm with him on this one," Breck said, with an apologetic glance at Leannán. "She's a witch woman. She'll be fine. She'll figure out a way out of this mess. And hopefully we'll be long gone by the time she does."

Leannán tied off the bandage on Prion's leg and stood. "We can't just leave her. Perhaps if we can get her out, she'll help us after all?" It was a long shot, but Leannán knew they had to do something.

She looked at Prion and put a hand on his arm. He glared at it but didn't shake it off. "We can't just leave her at his mercy. We have to try."

Prion pursed his lips and clenched and unclenched his jaw. After several long moments, he ground out, "Fine. But we only try once. And only after you're safely off this ship."

Leannán raised her eyebrows at him. "Once *I'm* off? I don't mean to be indelicate, but I'm the one who can escape the most easily here. Neither of you can dive overboard and swim away. How about we wait until you're off-ship, and then I try to convince her?"

Prion's face was thunderous. "No, absolutely not. I'm not risking you any further, especially not for the likes of her. I try to break her free or nobody does. We can risk the consequences with Adair later."

Breck looked thoughtful. "It will take us a few minutes to get the rowboat ready to take us over. I can buy you a few minutes. But you'll have to be fast."

"I can be fast," Prion promised. "Just get her off the ship as soon as you can. If I can manage to get to the *Tempest* in time, can you outsail *The Hellion*?"

"On a clear day with no breeze," Breck returned with a grin.

"Then get Leannán off the ship. If I can free the *buidseach*, I'll do so, then jump overboard and swim to you before they know we're gone."

"I don't like this," Leannán said, crossing her arms over her chest. "You can barely even walk on that leg."

"They won't come after me," Prion said reassuringly. "I'm a nobody in uncharted waters. Adair's men won't come in after me, because they're too worried about the things in the water."

"*I'm* too worried about the things in the water," Leannán protested. "We don't come here—we don't know what's lurking about."

"I'll be fine. Just stick to the plan."

"This is a dumb plan," Leannán said mulishly.

Prion limped close to her, ignoring Breck's sudden interest in anywhere but at the two of them. He put his forehead down to touch hers and smiled at the sudden hitch in her breath. "We'll be fine. I'll be fine. Besides, it won't matter if that *buidseach* refuses to help me. Then I come along with you. We'll make Harper safe, and I'll get my skin back and everything will be fine."

Prion smiled at her, then kissed her gently. She let herself melt into the sensation of his lips pressed against hers, let her body mold itself to his as his arms came around her. This, this was where she needed to be, her body cried. Right here, in his arms.

Breck cleared his throat. "I don't mean to interrupt, but I think I hear footsteps on the stairs. It's time."

Leannán reluctantly stepped back and saw nothing but loving reassurance in Prion's expression when he looked at her. He truly believed this would work. And it broke her heart. What did that mean for her if it all did work out?

The door opened and Bryce stepped in. "Ok, lady and gentlemen, it's time to head up. The Captain would like a word with you."

"We're ready," Prion said in a flat voice and walked out of the cargo hold. Breck gave her a sympathetic glance as he followed.

Please let it all work out, she told herself as she walked out of the hold and up the stairs to the top deck. *Please let Harper see there's no other way.*

CHAPTER 12

ON TOP OF THE deck, Adair waited for them near the railing. Prion noticed he had changed out of his wet clothes and into dry ones. When they approached, he turned and favored them with a winsome smile, as if they were honored guests aboard his ship instead of captives.

"My friends," he began, throwing his arms wide.

Breck coughed something that sounded like, "Bastard," and Adair's smile slipped.

"I've been thinking," he continued, ignoring the jab, "and I believe you were there to get help for your wretched situation. Which pains me, really." He adopted an expression of grotesque sympathy.

Prion wanted nothing more than to punch him in his perfect face.

"I've decided to let you go back to that little rig you sailed in on." Beside him, Breck bristled, but

Prion put a firm hand on his forearm and the man quieted. "And you can continue with your wreck of a honeymoon. I hope you can at least salvage some of it." He gave Leannán a nod to include her in his condolences. It pleased Prion to see her roll her eyes.

Breck nodded with a grim smile. "Of course, we won't mention this. Who would believe us? Bulls snorting fire? Magic portals? Witch women?" He snorted. "I'd not like to be the laughingstock of Selbane any time soon. I have a reputation to uphold."

"Good!" Adair gushed. "Then we have an understanding?" He looked expectantly at Leannán and Prion.

"We're not from Selbane, so we have no reason to spread rumors," Leannán demurred. "We'll be getting back to Laffton as soon as we can."

Adair's eyes narrowed. "Laffton? I thought you said you were from Lochton."

Prion froze. So close to being free and this was where they slip up?

But Leannán began coughing harshly, holding a fist to her mouth and bending over at the waist. Adair frowned and stepped forward to pat her on the back. After several hacking coughs, she straightened with a gasp. "Ugh! This sea air doesn't agree with me! I took in a bad breath at the wrong moment." She cleared her throat. "I meant to say

Lochton, of course." She smiled at Adair, who gave her an uncertain answering smile.

"Of course," he said in a doubtful tone. "I'm sure you'll be glad to get back." He snapped his fingers at the twins, who jumped to attention. "Men? If you'll prepare the boat for our guests' departure?"

The men moved to the railing and began fiddling with ropes. Breck gave Prion a pointed look, then moved forward to help them, calling, "Oh, lads, you've got those ropes crossed! Who taught you how to tie a proper knot?"

Prion turned to Adair. "Captain, if you don't mind, I believe I left our belongings in the cargo hold. Would you mind if I darted down to retrieve them?"

Adair frowned. "Nonsense. I can send Harris—" He turned to call the tall man, who was working at the other end of the ship.

But Prion laughed and shook his head. "There's no need to bother him. He looks busy. I can take care of it. I'll be back in a breath." Then he turned and darted down the stairs leading below-deck.

He paused at the bottom of the stairs, then turned down hallway opposite of the cargo hold. She had to be somewhere near here. He just hoped she was conscious now and able to talk.

He did not know what he was going to do to free her, but he figured she might help with that once he got there.

"Harper!" he hissed as he jogged down the hallway.

"Lord Prion?"

He stopped. The voice had come from the last doorway on his left. He backtracked and pushed the door open. There was Harper, tied to a chair behind a large wooden desk. So they'd put her in the Captain's office for the time being.

With a glance over his shoulder to make sure nobody had followed, he closed the door behind him and circled around behind her. Her hands were tied so tightly they were turning red from lack of circulation.

"They aren't taking any chances with you," he murmured. He bent to unfasten the knots.

"Why are you here?" she asked in a groggy voice.

"To help you," Prion lied.

"To make me help you," she countered. Prion rolled his eyes as he fiddled with the ropes. They were impossibly tight, and he was having no luck with them.

"Well, the thought had crossed my mind," he admitted. He paused and leaned around to look her in the face. There was a dark bruise at her temple and blood crusted at a cut on her lower lip. But though her voice sounded dazed, her eyes were clear and blazed at him.

"Help *you*?" she asked incredulously. "After you brought that man down on me?"

"I didn't know he was following us!" Prion exclaimed. "He just showed up!"

"After you and that woman let him in!"

Prion glared at her. "Leave Leannán out of this. She did nothing wrong."

"Because of her and you, I'm in this predicament!" Harper spat. "I wouldn't help you now if you were the last selkie in the sea!"

Prion froze. "So you could help fix my skin, you just are refusing to," he said.

Her angry glare didn't waver. It was answer enough.

He stood, feeling drained of all emotion. He stepped around her so that the desk stood between them. Placing his hands on the desk for support, he leaned forward so they were on eye level. "You never intended to help me, did you? No matter what I said? Nothing I did would get your assistance."

"That skin is beyond my repair—" Harper began, but Prion cut her off with a slash of his hand through the air.

"That's not what you said." He spoke in a low, rough voice. "That's not the reason you gave." He straightened and backed towards the door until his back bumped it. He groped blindly for the doorknob without looking at it. His eyes were on Harper.

Her angry expression changed as she realized he was leaving. Her face turned desperate, and she leaned as far forward as her ropes would allow. "You can't leave me here! Help me!" she cried.

"I wouldn't help you if you were the last selkie in the sea," he said softly. Then he turned the knob and left.

He blundered down the hallway, remembering at the last second that he came down to get their bags containing their sealskins. *So stupid!* he thought. How could he have forgotten those... again?

Not that it matters, a small, empty voice spoke up. His sealskin was still ruined beyond repair. Nothing could change that now.

He started up the stairs with the bags hanging in one fist against his leg. He didn't have the energy to pull them onto his back. When he arrived above-deck, the first thing he saw was Leannán, waiting near the railing. When she noticed him, she gave him an anxious, inquiring look that turned to confusion and then sadness as she realized he was alone. For him to be alone must have meant he'd failed.

She tried to take his hand as he passed her, but he ignored the attempt. The bustle of the crew seemed muted, the sounds softer, the colors of the sails and the sky dimmer than before. He registered Leannán saying his name, but he ignored it. He limped to the railing and peered over to see Breck waiting at the oars as the rowboat bobbed close to the ship. Breck motioned for him to toss down the bags, so Prion did, not caring if they made it safely down.

He was past caring. There was a vast emptiness inside him, a roaring that couldn't be contained that just said *gone, gone, gone.*

Leannán put a hand on his arm and led him to the opening in the railing so he could climb down. He went down the ladder fastened to the side of the ship, then sat back against the wet wood as Breck helped Leannán follow behind him. He ignored Breck's angry look, a look that implied that he, Prion, should help Leannán instead, but Prion just looked out at the ocean he would never swim in again and let the sound of the roaring water swallow him up.

CHAPTER 13

Back on the *Tamed Tempest*, Breck set about with Jack to make her sailable. Jack was full of questions about their trip and could tell they were despondent, but Breck brushed him aside.

"All answers in due time, lad," he said briskly, then directed Jack to pull up anchor and ready the sails. The wind was blowing in hard from the southeast, which would give them good time back to Selbane, Leannán thought.

Once on deck, Prion ignored everyone and walked below-deck. Leannán watched him walk away, saw the dejected set to his shoulders, and hesitated. He had been silent the entire boat ride back, staring out at the water with a blank expression on his chiseled face, his hands quiet in his lap, cradling the bag that held his sealskin. Any attempts to talk to him were met with silence.

Would he want company after this fiasco? And if she went, what would she say? All the things that popped into her head seemed lackluster, empty. How did she properly convey sympathy without it appearing as pity?

But her heart ached to see him like this. It broke a small part of her to see him so faded and without hope. If she could help him, even a little, didn't she owe it to him to try? The True Mate bond called for her to rush after him, to pull him into her arms and help him forget the bad news.

She gave in to the urge.

She followed him below-deck, guessing that he was headed to the Captain's quarters to be alone.

Prion stood just inside the door of the room. She took in the sight of her man, standing with bowed shoulders as if the weight of the surrounding air was too much to bear. She couldn't stand to see him so dejected, so broken. Crossing the threshold, she put a tentative hand on his shoulder.

When he didn't shrug her off, she stepped forward to press her chest against his back, laying her cheek on the curve of his shoulder blade. "We'll get through this," she murmured against his shirt.

"We?" Prion's voice was vague, as if he were a sleeper waking from a dream.

Leannán pulled on his shoulder until he turned to face her. "Of course, 'we!' We will find a way. Someone out there must know of a—"

"There is no fix for this, Leannán." His voice was weary. He wouldn't meet her eyes. "I am bound to the human life for the rest of my days. Without a skin, I can't—"

"We'll find you a new skin!" Leannán exclaimed. Her eyes widened with the intensity of the idea. The words began tumbling out of her mouth so fast her lips almost couldn't keep up. "We'll find a new one and you'll be able to shift again. All we have to do is—"

"Kill another selkie to do it." Prion's voice was gentle as he put his hands on her arms to stop her from speaking. "I won't do that, Leannán. I just won't. I won't let someone give up their life for me, just so I can feel the sea on my fur again."

Leannán's eyes filled with tears. "But to be lost to the water... forever..." It was a thought she could barely comprehend. It filled her with such dread, she didn't know how he was still alive to withstand it. She thought if she were in his position, she'd throw herself into the sea and let the water take what was rightfully its own, return to the waters that made her. But he was made of stronger stuff than she was, she realized. He would never sacrifice a life, his own or someone else's.

"You're still a Prince," she whispered. "The clan will take care of you."

"I am nothing to the clan. Not anymore."

"Lies!" Leannán exploded. "The clan is lost without you! You're the heir to the throne."

Now she could see fire sparking behind Prion's eyes as he scowled at her. "Do you think I'm unaware of my value to the clan now? What can a human offer a group of selkies? What possible advantage could I have now? Who would follow a broken leader, a banished Prince?"

Leannán recoiled. "Nobody banished you. Your mother, Mairi, she would never let—"

"I banish myself, Leannán. Here. Now." Prion straightened his shoulders, and she saw a glimmer of steel in his eyes. "I am nothing to the clan forevermore." He took a deep breath. "As I am nothing anymore to you."

Leannán let her hands fall to her side. "What are you saying?"

Prion turned away. "I don't blame you, Leannán, if that's what you're worried about. I understand the situation I find myself in. Perhaps too well. I expect nothing further from you. You tried your best to help me. Return to the clan and live your life."

Suddenly she couldn't keep it to herself anymore.

"I'm leaving," she said.

Prion frowned. "What do you mean?"

"After we got your skin fixed. I was going to..." She took a deep breath, "I've been planning it for some time now. I'm going to another clan."

Prion's eyes blazed as his face hardened. "Why would you do that? It's the only home you've ever known!"

"It was," she agreed, her expression wretched. "Until you... until I couldn't..."

"Couldn't what?"

"Watch you live the life you were living," she ground out. "I can't... there's no place for me there anymore. There never was."

"Don't do this now," Prion growled, stepping towards her with outstretched arms, as if intending to embrace her. "You can still have a life there."

But she stepped back, out of his reach. "This is for the best." She felt as if her heart were breaking. "But," she added hopefully, "maybe I can find someone in another clan who can help you. Maybe someone else has an answer..." She trailed away as Prion stared at her in shock. She willed herself not to react to the betrayal she saw in his eyes, the hurt that called to her, as his True Mate, to comfort him. It would only take one step.

She couldn't bear it.

She stepped forward, just as he closed his eyes and turned away.

"I don't need anyone. I'm on my own."

"Only because you are decreeing it to be so. But I can still help you. I—"

Now he rounded on her, the fury in his face sealing her lips before the rest of the words could emerge. "What, Leannán? What can you do? You took me to the selkie witch, and she couldn't... *wouldn't...* help me. What more do you think you, a handmaid, can do now? What can you do that a Prince cannot?"

She narrowed her eyes, one hand sliding up to press her fist between her breasts. "How dare you? How dare you push me away when all I want is to help you?"

"Why?" he hollered. "I'm nothing! I'm no better than a human now! Why do you want to help me?"

"Because I love you!"

For a moment, they stared at each other in shock, both wide-eyed and breathing heavily. Leannán thought her heart might burst from her chest from the force of its beating. Where had those words come from? And why did they choose that moment to tumble out of her mouth?

She'd known her feelings for him had been growing as the True Mate developed with their closeness. And she'd figured he'd felt it, too, and had pushed it aside for the sake of his quest. But to say it now, when he was at his most vulnerable, to make herself so vulnerable, too... It was a risky move that she wished she could take back.

But she held on to the glimmer of hope inside her, the part of her soul that called to his, that trembled under the thought of his touch. Would he say it back? Could he?

The emotions flitted across his face like lightning strikes: the shock that turned to fear that faded into... nothing. His face closed itself off, turning to granite before her eyes, and she watched in horror as all emotion slid from his face until he faced her, expressionless.

"I'm sorry," he breathed. "But there's no place for you here." He turned, giving her his back, and walked over to the bed. Without a word, he pulled the covers back, lay down with his back to her, and pulled his knees to his chest.

Tears burned her eyes, tumbling in fat drops down her cheeks unchecked. She stood, trembling, fists at her side, as she tried to replay the last thing he'd said. Not "I love you, too," as she'd been so certain he would. But "there's no place for you here."

A denial.

A rejection.

A betrayal.

Her lips pressed into a thin line in her face as she whirled and fled for the door. She snatched the satchel containing her sealskin from the floor next to it and tumbled out the door, leaving it open behind her. She fled for the sea, her emotions a swirl of chaos and hurt. Without realizing what she was doing, she ripped the bag open and pulled out her skin. Tossing the bag aside, she clenched her skin in her teeth as she ripped her clothes off, nearly tumbling to the ground as her pants got hung up on one leg.

She reached the top deck and heard Jack's startled exclamation as she raced, half-naked, towards the edge of the ship.

She pulled her shirt free as she reached the railing and threw herself into the air over it. Flinging the sealskin over herself as she went, she hooked the fasteners at her stomach with numb fingers that moved by instinct alone as she soared through the air, then plunged into the water's shocking coolness.

She curled into the change as her head dunked beneath the incoming waves, and she gave herself over to the sensations, the pleasure and pain of it more welcome than ever as it helped dull the pain of Prion's betrayal.

She swam without direction, not knowing where she was headed, just knowing she needed to get away from the rage, get away from the bed where they'd shared that night of beautiful memories, get away from the one who hurt her.

Never had she longed to be a true seal more than now. Oh, to never feel like this, this depth of emotion that cut her insides like knives. She felt her heart might burst from the sharpness of it, that her skin would be flayed from her body in its rawness. She swam blindly, not caring where she went, only knowing that she could never return.

CHAPTER 14

Prion could just make out the *Tamed Tempest* as it sailed down the shoreline towards the dock further in the town of Selbane. At Prion's request, Breck had dropped him at the ramshackle house that had started the whole mess. He knew Breck must have been eager to get him off his ship and even more eager to part him from the extra gold Prion tossed him to keep his mouth shut about what he'd seen.

"Like I told Adair, who'd believe me?" Breck said with a rueful grin. "I'm just happy I still have my skin about me." Then he'd realized the impact of what he said and his face fell. "Prion, I didn't—"

"It's fine," Prion lied as he turned away. "Be safe, Breck." He gave a half-hearted wave over his shoulder and walked down the ramp onto the sea grass-covered land a few yards down from the house. Then, shielding his eyes from the setting sun, he'd watched the *Tamed Tempest* sail away, back towards the town.

He stood there long after the *Tempest* was out of sight, relishing the last sunset he'd ever truly appreciate. This was his first day as a human, not a selkie stuck in a human body. From here out, he would live as a human, try to eke out a living as a human, and die in this human form as an old, withered man.

It was a damn depressing thought.

What made it even more depressing was the knowledge that he would never see Leannán again. His heart felt like it was only half-beating without her around. It longed for him to hold her, even one last time, to feel her skin pressed against his, to smell the scent of her hair as he pressed his nose to her head. It ached for her in a way he never could have imagined. In a short time, she had become all-consuming, a constant presence that he felt a physical ache to be near again. He realized this must be what love felt like, the desire for someone else that surpassed all other desires, something that touched his soul, not just his body.

But she deserved better. She deserved a new life in a new clan as she'd wanted. Now that he'd cut her loose, she was free to pursue the life she always wanted. She could make her own decisions.

He wished he could tell his heart the same thing.

As the sun set on the horizon, he turned his back on the lavender and orange streaks racing across the sky and went into the house. He would have his work cut out for him to make it habitable, he knew. But, as his damaged soul cried out, all he had was time.

Leannán didn't know how she ended up back at the Queen's personal chamber, but she suddenly realized where she was after swimming back through the underwater channel and emerging into the warm stone cave. She changed, crying, wiping her tears away as she pulled the sealskin from her bare back. Between her breasts, the icy chill of the ring burned her skin like a brand, so she ripped it away, heedless of the torn cord, as she slipped it over her finger.

"What is the matter, Leannán?" a kind voice asked behind her.

She whirled, wide-eyed, wiping her cheek with the heel of one hand. "My Lady, what are you doing here? I would have thought you'd retired for the night with King Righ."

Queen Mairi sat naked in a padded chair in front of an ornate gold mirror atop a wooden table. She smoothed her dark hair over one shoulder and set down a brush backed with mother-of-pearl onto the table.

"You thought you'd be alone?" Queen Mairi asked with a crooked eyebrow. "I can leave, if you'd like...?" A small smile played around the corners of her mouth.

Leannán clapped her fist to her heart and bowed, letting her wet hair slide off one shoulder. "I would never ask my Queen such a request."

"I should be retired for the night," the Queen admitted with a sigh, "But I felt... distressed. This whole mess with the sirens has kept me up most nights. As I suspected, the siren king and queen are backing their son and refuse to hear our pleas for justice. They actually hold that he was elsewhere when the attack was committed, despite our own Anchor witnesses." She snorted in derision. "I fear for our people should war break out." Her gaze sharpened on Leannán. "But if you're here, that must mean your journey is over."

When Leannán nodded sadly, the Queen stood in a fluid motion and strode over to her. She put her hands on Leannán's shoulders and pulled her over to a soft couch set against the stone wall of the chamber. "What happened? Where is Prion? Tell me everything."

Leannán sniffed, unwilling to speak and unsure of where to start. But the Queen rose again before she could begin and retrieved her hairbrush from the table. Sitting once more, she turned Leannán so that her back was to the Queen, and then began to brush Leannán's wet hair, working the tangles carefully with her fingers.

"Start at the beginning," Queen Mairi suggested in a gentle voice.

Leannán closed her eyes against the flood of emotions that raced through her at the Queen's kind words. She took a deep breath, letting the Queen's ministrations soothe her, and then began, starting with hiring Breck to take them out to Little Krill Island.

As she spoke, Queen Mairi stayed silent. She continued to brush, using her fingers to untangle the small snarls in Leannán's hair, and soon Leannán felt a softness steal over her, a peace that made it seem as if she were talking to herself.

She felt the Queen's fingers pause when she admitted the True Mate bond, but otherwise the Queen said nothing, simply stroked and pressed the brush tines over her scalp in firm, strong strokes. When her hair was untangled, the Queen began to plait it into small braids starting at either temple.

"—And then he sent me away," Leannán concluded. Her voice caught at the last word, breaking the way her heart felt that it had already done. The Queen finished braiding in silence, letting her strong fingers weave the smaller braids together into a large one. When she was done, she patted the braid, seeming satisfied with her work, and pulled on Leannán's shoulder to turn her towards her.

Leannán was afraid to look at the Queen, afraid to see the judgment that must surely be there. She'd given her heart to someone who was untrustworthy, and she deserved the pain she had received. She knew this was what the Queen would say, and though she knew it was the truth, she still dreaded to hear it. When the Queen spoke, her words were final, and Leannán knew hearing her voice say it would cement the pain forever in her heart.

"My son doesn't deserve you," Queen Mairi said, running her finger across the arc of Leannán's eyebrow and down along her jaw. When Leannán met her gaze in surprise, she smiled. "To be gifted the love of your True Mate is a boon indeed, and he was not smart enough to understand what he was being given. He doesn't deserve you or your gift."

"But he does!" Leannán burst out, shocked. "He is kind and strong and generous. He has given everything he has for this mission—"

"But what did he give you?" Queen Mairi broke in.

Leannán paused. Only the most incredible night of her life. Only the feeling, finally, of coming home, of knowing that she'd found the one true place her heart wanted to be and that she could stay there as long as she'd wanted. At least that was how it had felt, laying in his arms that night. As if the world could go on forever and she could remain where she was, safe and loved.

But this was too big to say to the Queen, and she didn't know the words. She looked down at her hands crumpled in her lap instead. Prion's ring twinkled in the dim light around the edges where the silver was like tiny, twisted wire.

"And there was this," Leannán whispered, raising the knuckle that wore the ring.

The Queen touched it reverently, then used her finger to lift Leannán's chin until their eyes met. Her smile was serene, as if oblivious to the turmoil in Leannán's heart and soul. "My son loves you, Leannán. How could you not see this? He gave you his heart. HOw could you not see it?"

"How do you know this?" Leannán asked in surprise.

"Because I know my son. He may have told you to go, but if he gave you that ring, he loves you. He would sooner risk his life than part with that thing. It meant the world to him. It was the last memorial he had of his grandsire."

Leannán nodded. "Yes, he told me that. But he said nothing of love when he gave it to me. Just that I was to return it to you."

A line appeared between the Queen's eyebrows. "I could never take it. It's not meant to be worn by me. It's a gift for a True Mate, to be given when he felt the time was right. Why do you think he's never given it up before?"

"Because he's never been in love before?" A spark of hope blossomed in her heart. If he loved her, was there a chance?

Queen Mairi nodded. "Not until now, I'd say."

Leannán looked back down at the ring, marveling at this new information. As the Queen rose from the couch, she frowned. "But what do I do now? He thinks I'm leaving for a new clan."

The Queen raised her eyebrows in surprise. "But why would you do that, my dear? Your home and your heart are here."

"My heart is with him," Leannán said softly.

Queen Mairi smiled. "Then go to him. Show him. Teach him what it's like to be truly loved and deserving of love. I think that's one lesson he has yet to learn."

Leannán smiled, and it felt like sunlight breaking through a storm. The lightness in her heart and body flooded her with purpose. She could show him love. She could heal his heart, even if she hadn't been able to help heal his sealskin.

But first she had to find him. He'd been on Breck's ship the last time she'd seen him. He could be on his way to anywhere in the world by now. Her smile faded. "How do I find him?"

The Queen thought for a moment. "I'd go to the last place you spent time with him. He's a creature of habit, my son. He'll return to what he knows."

Leannán rose, wiping at the salt on her cheeks from the dried tears. "Thank you, my Lady. I—"

"Go," the Queen said with a smile.

Leannán went.

CHAPTER 15

THERE WAS A KNOCK at the door.

"Go away," Prion growled, as he straightened an old wooden armoire that had been sitting in the corner of the room. It was missing a foot and sat at a drunken angle, but he'd propped it up with a chunk of stone he'd found outside and now it canted a little less drunkenly than it had before. He stared at it critically. He was going to have to figure out how to fix that properly, but at the moment, the concept was just too daunting.

Another knock sounded, harder this time.

"I said go away!" he shouted. It was probably Breck, who was the only one who knew where he was, and he wasn't in the mood for company. It had been days since Breck had dropped him on the island at this ramshackle house, and he was determined to make it habitable. After all, it was where he had resigned to stay for the rest of his life.

He knew he was free to go anywhere, be anybody he wanted to be, but at the moment, he was just tired. Little tasks seemed too large, and he'd had a hard enough time keeping himself bathed—fixing up the house had seemed like too much.

That, topped with the fact that he hadn't eaten in three days, made life seem even more overwhelming. Soon he would have to figure out how to survive as a human, which meant getting money to buy food. Unless he could figure out how to fish for himself, which was the most likely—

Another loud banging at the door, hard enough to make it rattle in its frame. If they kept that up, the whole thing might fall off and how much effort would *that* cost to fix?

He strode towards the door. "Breck!" he yelled. "I said go—"

He ripped the door open and came face-to-face with a scowling Leannán.

Without a word, she brushed past him, knocking her shoulder into his chest to move him aside.

"Leannán, wha—"

"I found Breck," she said without preamble. "He told me where to find you."

Prion scowled. "He had no business telling you that."

"Why did you give me this?" Leannán demanded, ignoring his question as she whirled to hold up her hand with the ring on it. She held her fist dangerously close to his face, and he wondered if she meant to punch him.

He stared at her. "Because I..."

"Because you what? I want to hear you say it." She took a step forward, and he retreated a so that his back hit the wall next to the door.

"I gave it to you because I wanted my mother to know—"

"Wrong! She would have known I wouldn't return without you if I'd abandoned you. That would be paramount to a death wish!"

"I thought you were going to another clan anyway!" he rallied with a scowl. He slammed the door behind him and took a step towards her. "You were leaving! Why shouldn't I try to protect you? If you'd left me and my parents found you without that ring—"

"But I didn't leave you!" she exclaimed. Her expression pleaded with him to understand. "You sent me away."

He threw his arms wide to indicate the world outside the house. "To make your own decisions. To live your own life!"

"Because you love me."

"Of course because I love you!" He scowled at her, ignoring her round eyes and shocked, open mouth. "How could I act any other way? I learned some things on that island, some truths about myself. And one of them was that I am not enough for you. I barely got you out of danger from that bull, couldn't do anything to protect you other than tell you to run."

"But you did protect me—" Leannán started, but Prion cut her off as if she hadn't spoken.

"I learned that you are more important to me that anything else in my life. And because of that, I release you. I release you to live the life you deserve to have."

Leannán took a step toward him. "But don't you see you deserve that life, too?" she said softly. She reached out a hand to him and he looked away with an angry scowl. He didn't deserve her, he knew. How could he make her understand he was broken beyond repair? That he didn't deserve someone as steadfast and loyal as her?

"You do," Leannán pressed on, taking another step towards him. She placed a gentle hand on his forearm. He didn't pull away, but he couldn't meet her eyes. "You protected me from that bull, took a blast that was meant for me. You saved my life, Prion."

He looked down at his damaged leg, and it seemed to be more proof of his ruin than anything else. "And you think you owe me something because of that?"

Leannán squeezed his arm and he looked up at her. The tenderness in her eyes was heartbreaking, and he couldn't stand to see it directed at him. Not when he didn't deserve it. "I owe you nothing. But I love you too much to let you stay in this hole you've dug for yourself."

At that, he turned to face her and looked her directly in the eyes. "Dug for myself? That *buidseach*, that witch... she refuses to help me and you say I dug *myself* in this hole?" His voice cracked with incredulity.

But Leannán met his eyes evenly, without judgment. "You banished yourself. And you sent me away. Prion, you have the means to turn this around. You just have to accept that you are not some broken, irredeemable soul. You have value, and you deserve to have love."

She let go of his arm and reached up to pull the ring necklace from around her neck. "Why did you give me this?" she asked quietly, bowing her head to stare down at the ring in her hands.

Prion stared at it, confused. Why was she circling back around to this now? "Because..." The words stuck in his throat. To say them, to make them real... "Because you are my True Mate."

She nodded, not meeting his eyes. It shocked him to see a tear fall from her eyes onto her palm, bathing the ring in wetness and making it gleam in the dim light. He had never seen her cry before.

"But why give it to me? Why not keep that knowledge to yourself? Nothing said you had to acknowledge it."

Prion took a steadying breath. "Because I needed to take care of you in case something went wrong in the caves."

Another tear fell, and Prion had the horrible sinking feeling that he'd given the wrong answer. What did he have to say to make her feel better? She didn't deserve to be brought to tears, by him or anyone. He struggled with how to make it right, how to give her what she needed

The truth, a small voice in the back of his mind said. *She needs the truth.*

He took in her bowed head and inhaled deeply, steeling himself. "And..." He paused.

Did her head raise just a little? Was she waiting for his answer? Could he make this better?

"And I love you, Leannán. I can't image a time without you by my side. And in that moment, I just felt like... like you had given me so much of yourself. And I had given you nothing in return."

Leannán raised her head and peered at him with a small frown. But she remained silent, as if waiting for more.

He took another deep breath. He could give her more.

"You deserve to know how much you mean to me. You deserve so much more than what I can give you, but I had to give you something, even the tiniest token I was capable of, to show you how much I cared."

"Cared?" Her voice was flat, inflectionless.

"Not cared. I still do." His expression pleaded with her to understand. "I cannot give you what you need. I am..." He couldn't find the words, had failed again to convey even the simplest of emotions. Anger burned in him at his incompetence.

"You are my everything," Leannán whispered. He turned shocked eyes on her. "Where you see damage and brokenness, I see strength and kindness. Sacrifice. Heart." Her eyes were like twin lights, pulling him in so that he could not look away. "You are the strongest person I have ever met. And I love you so truly, so deeply, Prion. Nothing can change that. And if you want me to leave..." She took a deep, shuddering breath.

Without thinking, he blurted out, "But I don't." He stepped forward and put his forehead to hers. "I don't want a life without you, Leannán. But I fear I can't give you what you deserve."

"You are everything I deserve," she whispered, holding his gaze. Her warm breath kissed his lips. "And everything I want." She pulled back with a suddenly fierce gaze. "But I'll tell you what I don't want."

Prion braced himself. This was where she laid out his deficiencies. Here was where she told him how he wasn't good enough...

"I don't want anyone less than you. I want you with all your flaws. All your brokenness. And I promise I will help you heal them. But you can't shut me out. Not again. Let me in. Let me love you like you deserve to be loved."

He paused and stared at her in shock. His eyes were wide, and his mouth dropped open in a small O. "I don't deserve you, Leannán." His voice was hoarse with emotion.

Leannán smiled at him, and it was like the sun breaking through dark clouds. She was glorious in her radiance. "My love, you deserve the world."

"I love you," he said reverently, carefully, as if the words might still repel her out of the door and out of his arms. "Oh gods, I—"

"And I adore you," she said, throwing herself forward into his arms. He pulled her closer, pressing his face into her hair and inhaling her scent.

This.

This was what it was like to come home.

His hands pressed against her, pushing her back to make room for him to speak. So much of what he'd felt on the island came rushing back to him and he wanted to tell her all of it.

But instead, she stood on tiptoe and pressed her lips against his, kissing him so deeply that he forgot what he was about to say, forgot everything but the intense emotion raging through him at her nearness.

She loves me, he thought as he kissed her back, tasting and sliding his tongue against hers. *This is what love tastes like.* It was salt and sea and Leannán.

Then he was crashing onto the bed, and he didn't even know where his shirt had gone.

There was a loud crack, and the bed fell beneath them, dropping them with a jarring thump. They looked at each other in surprise, then down at the bed. One leg had given way and now the bed tilted them at an angle.

"I always knew this thing would give out at the wrong time," Prion muttered, and Leannán gave him a questioning look. "Never mind," he mumbled as he reached for her, and she pressed her shirtless body to his.

He flipped her over and pulled her trousers off in a smooth motion, then shucked out of his own. His erection caught the edge of his waistband, then rose proud and free in the cool air. She stared at him for a moment, then smiled.

It was a warm, welcoming smile, and he answered by pressing his body against hers, skin-to-skin, letting his firm length push against her tender juncture.

"I want you now, Prion," she murmured into his mouth as he kissed her. "Now and forever."

"Forever," Prion answered. It sounded like the perfect amount of time.

He pushed her thighs aside and slid into her, marveling at the slickness, the tightness that pressed against him like a glove. "You're so wet!" he moaned, and her lips twisted into a smile. She pulled him close to her, crushing her breasts against his chest as he began to move in her, slowly at first, then faster as the sensations built inside him.

"Leannán," he ground out, moving to lick and suck at the tender skin on her neck.

"My Prince," she moaned, as her hips thrust up to meet him, push for push and thrust for thrust as he glided in and out.

"Oh gods, Leannán, I'm close!"

Their cries of passion exploded at the same time as their climax crested over the both of them, drowning them in pleasure. Sparks burst throughout his mind as he came, and he became aware of two heartbeats pounding in rhythm, two sets of ragged breaths surging through his lungs. It was like their first time in the Captain's chambers aboard the *Tamed Tempest*, but better, fuller, richer. He realized he could sense the satisfaction radiating out from her, could sense, on an internal level, the bone-deep pleasure settling into her.

This is what it's like, he thought in wonder and felt an answering sense of surprise from her, like a cloudburst in his mind.

"Did you say something?" she asked languidly. He sent a mental sense of satisfaction at her and was delighted to see her shiver as the sensation hit her.

"What is this?" he asked in an awestruck voice. It was like a chord drawn between them, and through it he could feel her emotions as she felt them, though he couldn't sense her thoughts. He curled his body around her like a question mark and she made a murmur of appreciation that he felt in his body and his mind.

"The True Mate bond," she said. "It finally took hold, and it's beautiful."

"Like you," he breathed, kissing her neck as the realization set into place like a stone settling to the bottom of the sea. He would never be alone again, never searching for the other part of himself as he had been for so long, searching for that Leannán-shaped hole in his very soul. He was surprised with how peaceful he felt at the knowledge that they were truly True Mates, that they had come together finally after so long. No longer did he feel as if he wasn't enough for her—now he knew he would spend the rest of his life ensuring that he was, that he would live up to being the man she believed him to be.

She smiled up at him and sent an answering sensation of pleasure through their True Mate bond.

"And is it always like this?" he asked.

"How should I know?" she laughed. "It's a first for me, too."

It occurred to him that she didn't appear nearly as surprised at this as he was. He sat up on one elbow and looked down at her. "How long have you known?"

She gave him a languid smile and put one arm behind her head. "Since we were teens."

His eyebrows shot upward. "But we were kids then! Why didn't you say anything?"

She laughed. "And what would I have said? 'Guess what, even though we're ten, we're meant to be together forever'? It wasn't until we'd both matured that I knew for sure, and by then, we'd already started going our separate ways."

His expression turned serious as he trailed one finger down her jawline. "Never again." At her questioning look, he said, "We're never going our separate ways again. It's just us, forever."

"Forever," she returned with a smile.

Prion looked around at the bed in sudden interest, then gave her a mischievous smile. "What say we try to break the other legs, too?"

She grinned back at him and shifted so that she wrapped her legs around his waist. "I'm game if you are."

And he was.

CHAPTER 16

"Are you going to be okay?" Leannán asked Prion.

"If you're going to stay, I can't be too proud to avoid this," he said with a nervous sigh. "And I can't run from my responsibilities any longer." He took her hand and squeezed. "Those days are done."

They stood on the edge of the beach, near the waterline. It was near dusk and he wondered how long it would be until his parents appeared. They had agreed to meet him at sundown, and the sun was already a sliver on the horizon.

Beside him, Leannán shivered, and he quickly removed his cloak to place it around her shoulders. He felt a sliver of irritation at his parents for making them wait. They were known for being punctual, and this kind of delay was uncharacteristic of them.

"I'm going to have to get used to this," she admitted, pulling the cloak closed at her throat.

"The cloak?"

"Being cold all the time." That was how she described being human to him, and while it didn't affect him the same way, he had more muscle mass to keep him warm than she did.

He put his finger under her chin to turn her face towards him. He looked into her eyes. "You don't have to be like me," he assured her for the fifth time that day. "You can still change. You're not stuck to land like I am."

She smiled and covered his hand with hers. "I'm in this with you, regardless of my ability to change. I freely give that up. I want to truly be with you as you are." She kissed his knuckles. "I'm fine with this, really."

He opened his mouth to retort, but a seal barked from the water beyond them, and they turned to look at it. It barked again, then disappeared below the water.

"I suppose that means they're imminent," Prion said dryly.

Moments later, King Righ emerged from the water with Queen Mairi behind him. They wrapped their sealskins like cloaks around their bare shoulders, fastening them at the throat with clasps made of gold and pearls. Their long hair streamed water down their bodies, but they both wore the water as if it were fine garments.

"Mother, Father," Prion said, inclining his head at each of them.

"Your mother tells me you've made your decision," King Righ said with a frown. Queen Mairi shot him an irritated glance, then smiled indulgently at Prion as if to say *what can you do?*

Prion straightened his shoulders and lifted his chin. "I have. I will remain as a human for the rest of my days here, on Selbane."

King Righ studied him with a calculating look that made Prion fight to keep from squirming. *I am no young pup anymore,* he told himself. *I am the Prince, in name if nothing else. And I will bow to nobody.*

"You know Andara will take over as heir someday instead of you?" the King said, his voice rising in a slight question. "You're all right with that?"

"It's the only way," Prion said. "He'll make a fine King someday. He's seen every teacher I have and surpassed me in warrior training. And Trian after him, if necessary." Prion knew his two brothers would make strong candidates, certainly stronger than he'd ever shown himself to be, though he'd far surpassed them in war theory. It was the right thing, even if it did give him a pang of jealousy for what they had that he'd lost.

"How will you make a living?" King Righ asked in a curious voice.

"I have an answer to that," Queen Mairi spoke up. The King and Prion both turned to her with surprised expressions.

"You do?" Prion asked.

Queen Mairi smiled. "He will be a collector of rare sea artifacts and treasures. He can sell them to buyers on the island, or even on the mainland, if he so desires."

Prion exchanged a quick glance with Leannán. "And where will I get these treasures?"

"They will be brought to you," Queen Mairi said. "We will deliver shipments every week, small trinkets as we find them, treasure from sunken ships, pearls... other items humans find shiny and valuable. We can provide it to you, as retribution for your.... situation." She looked uncomfortable at that last, but collected herself visibly and pressed on. "As your new command dictates, you will need to be kept in good health and standing."

Prion frowned. "What new command?" It was like she was speaking a new language he didn't quite understand. Each new statement brought a new wave of confusion.

"Ah, yes, that," King Righ said, clearing his throat. Prion was shocked to see a slight blush working its way up his father's cheeks. "That was my idea." He straightened his shoulders and looked Prion directly in the eyes. "You are to be our Strategic Anchor Commander."

Prion felt his stomach drop with shock. His hand unconsciously spasmed in Leannán's hand. He felt her send a surge of courage and support through the True Mate bond, and it steadied him.

"—will provide direction to the Anchors for their duties," his father was saying.

"But... but why? How can I be of use to the clan when I'm stuck on land as a human?" Prion stammered.

"Like human generals direct their armies, so you will direct our Anchors. They will report to you regularly and you will instruct and command them to help protect our clan."

The thought that he could still be useful to the clan was a shock nearly as great as the new role he was being delivered. It would be possible, he realized, to advice and direct the Anchors without being in the water with them. And if war did break out between their clan and the sirens, he would still be able to send the Anchors where they were most needed, provided he received regular reports on their positions.

"I will need to know where the clan is at all times for this to work," he warned. "It's a risk."

"You were the best student in war theory," King Righ said with a small, proud smile. "You have more knowledge of strategy and defense than either of your brothers. You will be a great asset to the clan in this new role."

Prion felt his chest swell with pride. His father was proud of him. His father thought he was an asset, after all, despite all he'd shown himself to be. "I won't let you down," he said in a ringing voice.

Beside him, Leannán sent a surge of approval through the True Mate bond.

"I know you won't," Queen Mairi said with a smile. Then, taking King Righ's hand, they turned and slipped back into the water.

He watched them pull on their sealskins and change, sliding like silk into the water without a backward glance. The sight of it, of what he'd lost, tore at him, sending a flare of hot jealousy through him.

But Leannán sent a wave of comfort and peace, and it calmed him. He let her feelings wash over him, soothing his pain, and knew he was finally where he belonged.

He had finally come home.

EPILOGUE

FROM THE OTHER END of the couch, Prion heard Leannán growl.

The last days of fall had slipped away and winter had just started to take a firm grip on the island. The wind from the water was cut with ice, and it snuck through the cracks in the ramshackle house to whip around them in small breezes despite the warmth of the fire in front of them.

"What's the matter, love?" Prion asked in a distracted voice. He was poring over the latest ledger entry, painstakingly drawing the symbols for each item in the last shipment his parents had sent to him. They had come across a cache of black pearls, and he knew the jeweler in town would pay top price for the lot of them. He drew a crude circle with a stylus, mentally chafing again at the fact that he had to use human symbols for items instead of selkie runes.

"I can't get this material to play nice," Leannán growled back.

Prion glanced up to see her glaring down at her crochet needles as she wrestled with a particular stitch in the item she was making.

"I'm sure you'll get it," he said, turning back to his ledger.

cooperating!" Her needles rattled together with several angry clicks, and she collapsed the whole mess in her lap with a frustrated sigh.

Prion looked back at her. "What is that you're working on?" he asked, giving her his full attention for the first time. She seemed to be forming some kind of shoe out of wool, which seemed silly to him.

Leannán smoothed the hair from her face and gave him a coy sideways glance. "Oh, just a *little* something."

"A little something what? It looks like a sock."

Leannán's smile widened. "That's because it is."

Prion frowned. The satisfaction radiating through the True Mate bond was curious. "But it's too small."

"Is it?" Her voice was sly, teasing.

Prion's frown deepened as the satisfaction sense flared brightly. He was obviously missing something.

"Yes, as a matter of fact it is," he said, feeling irritated at the sense that he was the butt of some joke he didn't get. He set the ledger and stylus aside on the nearby table, then turned to her. "That won't fit either of us the way you're doing it."

"That's because it's not for us."

He gave her a nonplussed look. "Then who is it for? Some incredibly tiny, small person who isn't one of the two of... oh." He stopped, thunderstruck.

The True Mate bond flared like the sun in victory, and he suddenly realized what she was getting at.

He dropped to his knees on the carpet in front of her and took her hands in his. "Oh, gods, Leannán. Don't tell me we're going to... that you're..?" He cast an anxious look at her stomach. It still looked as flat as before... or did it?

She grinned down at him and nodded.

"How long have you known?" His hands reached for her stomach, sliding on either side of her belly as if it were fragile and easily hurt.

"I had my suspicions at the end of summer. But I wasn't sure until the autumnal equinox."

He leaned forward and kissed her belly, and she threaded her fingers through his hair. He lay his ear against her stomach, hearing the gurgles and rumblings as it churned. The True Mate bond didn't feel any different—it was still a glowing sense of whatever emotion she was feeling—but he felt like it should feel different, stronger somehow with the presence of another life.

"What will we call it?"

"If it's a boy, I want to name him Làidir. If it's a girl, Lyall."

He pulled back with a small frown. "That's awfully specific. How long have you been thinking about this?"

"Since the end of summer, silly," she said with a laugh.

He grinned at her and sent a wave of affection down the True Mate bond. "I can never get enough of you," he admitted, grinning up at her with a goofy smile, drunk on his love for her.

"Good thing you'll never have to."

He leaned forward and reached up to twine his fingers in her hair. Gently he pulled her head down to his. "Forever?" he murmured against her lips.

She answered his kiss with a gentleness that broke his heart all over again. "Forever."

Please feel free to leave a review for this book on Amazon and Goodreads!

Head to the next page for a free preview of *Stealing the Selkie's Heart*, available July 19, 2022!

FREE PREVIEW OF STEALING THE SELKIE'S HEART

Una MacCallan was not just a smart woman; she was what her husband used to call "wily." Too wily, he'd said, but that was neither here nor there now. She didn't see it as a negative, though he said it that way—to her, it meant she knew how to survive once he was gone, lost to sea only three years into their marriage.

She remembered the morning she'd found out, having arrived at her fish store on the edge of the harbor to find Walter Brown, deckhand on *The Harvester*, waiting for her. Behind him was a small group of people who had the watchful look of people who are trying not to be noticed but who want to be close enough to hear the conversation. They were too busy doing absolutely nothing, and she didn't like the look of it. People meddling in others' business was a sure way to tick her off.

So she'd met Walter with more aggression than she'd meant to. "Walter Brown, what are you doing hanging around my stand at this hour? You know I'm not open until mid-day." Her voice came out sharp, hard enough that he flinched and glanced uneasily over his shoulder at the group behind him. Una thought she saw several women lean surreptitiously closer.

"Mrs. MacCallan, I... I was sent..." He stammered to a halt, blushing and wringing his hands at his belt. "I mean to say—"

"Well then, say it!" she'd spat, and his blush deepened. Immediately she felt bad for making the young man upset, but she was in a hurry to get her fish supply from the docks, and she didn't have time for this fellow.

"There's been an accident."

Una's scowl slipped from her face in her surprise. There were accidents all the time on the open waters; it was the occupational hazard of being a fishing town. But nobody had ever bothered to inform her of them before; she always heard from them from local gossip from the women who came to her stand to buy fish.

"Blair." The word slipped from her lips, and even before the word was all the way out, Walter was nodding, looking grateful he didn't have to say anything further. Behind him, the crowd was staring, wearing equal expressions of shock and greed.

"His ship hit a reef a few hundred miles out, and… none of the men made it. Captain Campbell was the one who came across the wreckage late last night."

"How did they know it was the *Laguna*?"

"Pieces from the boat, ma'am. From the, you know…"

"The wreckage." Her voice sounded like it was coming from very far away. Dimly she registered the hushed whispers from the crowd, but inside her was a low hum. What was she going to do without Blair's income? Would she be able to survive? And then, on the tail end of that thought, *I should feel more than this*. It was true that their marriage was not one of love. Blair had been her sea captain father's beloved second-mate, and he'd been around their family since she was young. It had been natural to assume they'd be married someday—the entire town knew he was a good man, and his father couldn't imagine her with anyone else. So she'd said yes when he asked for her hand. She'd been happy with Blair, content even. But love? There was never room for that in their marriage. They'd both known it.

Una brushed her hair back from her face from where the cool wind of late afternoon had blown it into her eyes. So much had changed that day. How would her life have been different if Blair had returned to her? Would she still be selling fish for a meager profit down on the docks? Would the town have turned around for the better, or would the hard times that had come on when she was young still be continuing, as they were today? There was no way to know.

All she knew was that the mussels she was looking for would carry a good price at the fish market, if she could find enough of them. The town's big import was fish, and fishing was what the town was good at—catching them, processing them, feeding their families off it. The sea gave them everything. But not so many of them took the time for the smaller catches, the mussels, the codling and wrasse, the peeler crabs used for bait. That was where she cornered the market, hunting the hard-to-find locales to find the specialties enjoyed by some of the more successful of the islanders in Selbane. The mayor, in fact, had a weakness for mussels, and she expected to sell several pounds to the house servant who bought for him.

She made a mental note to herself to look back through her father's old journals again—though she'd pored over them after his death, she may have missed mention of some of his honey holes, the places where good catches always happened. They might help her later if this mussel adventure didn't play out the way she hoped.

She rubbed her palms together, noting how the rough edges scraped against each other. *This haul better be good*, she thought. Her month depended on it, given the lean times the town was going through.

She had found the cave a few weeks ago, back when she was scouting the shorelines in her small fishing boat for likely harbors for peeling crabs. It was secluded and close enough to the island's saltwater inlet that she bet she'd find plenty of mussels inside. But the water entrance had seemed too small, so she now beached her boat just outside the cave, amid a clump of sea grass to hide it from passing fishermen, and walked a short way past the cave to a rocky outcropping nearby. She'd found the small rocky area after she'd first found the cave and used the natural camouflage of the rocks to hide her mussel-gathering supplies, so she didn't have to haul them with her every time she visited.

Once she grabbed a bucket, she walked back to the cave, stepping around the sandy ground near the wall until she found the mouth entrance.

Inside was a wonder, with a high-arching ceiling of chipped gray stone. A small sandy beach dotted with tan and black pebbles lay at the mouth's edge, surrounded by large boulders that stood like a barrier against the water. She guessed she'd timed it perfectly, arriving during low tide—otherwise, she bet water would mostly fill the cave.

"I couldn't have docked my boat here anyway," she mused as she walked in, stepping carefully to avoid turning her ankle on the shifting sand. She moved to the far side of the cave, where the boulders were closest to the water's edge. Then, crouching down, she dipped her bucket in the water so she'd be able to keep the mussels alive during her trip back, and began hunting for the small black mussel shells she hoped she'd find dug into the side of the boulders. It was important to look for the right kinds: ones that looked clean, not too covered in barnacles, and of a medium size. Too small and they weren't worth the effort it took to prize the meat from inside.

She was in luck! Along the side of several of the boulders, she saw the black mussels sticking up like small mouths where the rocks were still wet. She set to work prying the mussels off with a sharp, twisting motion, grateful for her rough hands that worked better than any set of gloves she knew other fishermen sometimes wore.

She was busy ripping away the mussels when she heard a disturbance in the water, a live-sounding splashing noise. Peeking around the boulder, she hoped not to disturb whatever it was. She knew seals sometimes passed through here and knew they could be dangerous if a human encountered one up close. Still, the lovely creatures were a fascination for her, and she couldn't help but hope to see one up close.

And again, luck was on her side. A large gray seal, a male from the size of him, lumbered out of the water with a loud splash. She marveled at its size and the glossy head that looked left and right as it emerged, scanning the cave for enemies. Or food. She scooted the bucket of mussels further away from the water's edge. The last thing she needed was to lose her catch to some hungry animal.

As she watched, the seal dipped his head towards his belly, she assumed to scratch an itch. But then she saw the skin open, like a coat, revealing pink skin underneath. The seal's head slipped to one side to show a man's head, with gorgeously tousled red hair. His green eyes scanned the cave again, then one hand came up and swept the sealskin from his head as if brushing off a hat. Hands and knees appeared from underneath the sealskin, and then he was rising, naked and glorious, from the sand. The sealskin fell from his back as he stood and sighed.

Una froze in amazement. She knew the lore, probably better than most on the island having learned it all from her father, but to see a selkie in real life... It was incredible. She was watching her childhood stories come true, of men who wore sealcoats and swam in the ocean as an animal, only to come to shore as a human. Yes, she knew her history well, and even as her brain screamed at her that she was seeing magic in the flesh—and what tantalizing flesh it was—another part of her mind was plotting.

She remembered sitting at her father's feet, could still smell his pipe smoke as he talked, telling of the magical tale of how the selkie woman saved the town centuries ago, when the divide between humans and supernatural creatures wasn't so far apart. She remembered how her father described her, as fair as milk and with hair as dark as the sea, as she came forward and brought prosperity to the town. How she took a human husband and gave up the honey holes where fishermen caught boatfuls more than ever before. She had saved the town from ruin, back then, and wasn't it so unlikely that the town would need a savior now if it were to ever flourish again?

She watched the muscles in his fair skin flex, his abdominals contracting as he bent and gathered the sealskin from the water's edge and carefully folded it, placing it ever so gently on a rock to keep it safe.

Yes, she knew her lore. So she kept quiet, appreciating the view as the lean man turned and retrieved a bundle from the far wall. She watched him dress—with some disappointment—and stuff something into his pocket. Then he strode with purpose from the cave, off to whatever business he had on land.

She stayed where she was for a long time, wondering if she had the courage to do what she had planned. Could he be the key to saving the town? Could she tame him, bind him the way the lore said? She'd heard of selkie wives, how the men found the abandoned sealskin and kept it, binding the selkie women to them until they bore children, fey and bountiful, for them. Then they returned the skin and kept the children, letting the women fade back into the water whence they came.

She had no need of a selkie husband, that much was clear. But the town needed help. And if this selkie could tell them where to fish, the town could turn around, could prosper once more.

Rising, mussels momentarily forgotten, she stepped to the rock where the sealskin lay bundled on top of it. With gentle hands, she reached out, caressing the skin, feeling the silky, oily texture of the still-wet fur. It was like a fur coat, she told herself. There was no harm in touching it.

She picked it up, expecting to feel the heavy weight of it. But instead she felt a jolt, like lightning, run up her arms. Her fingers clenched in the skin, bunching the material in her fists. Something had happened. Something magical. Her fingertips still tingled from the electric jolt that had now faded to a slight prickle.

As if jolted into action, she moved quickly, folding the sealskin into a bundle. She looked around the cave for an alcove, an indentation, *somewhere* to hide the skin. She didn't know how long the selkie would be gone, and she needed the skin hidden when he returned. Without that leverage, he would have no reason to help her.

Then she remembered that she already had a hiding hole! Holding the wet sealskin to her chest, sopping the front of her dress, she ran out of the cave to the rocky outcropping where she hid her mussel-gathering buckets. She pulled the buckets out of the hole and carefully placed the sealskin in. Then, using her dress as an apron, she gathered some small stones to cover over the top of the skin.

When she was done, she stepped back and evaluated her work. It would hold. At a quick glance, the area appeared to be nothing more than a rocky outcropping, a natural rock formation in the ground itself. But if the selkie got closer, he would see through the holes that there was something underneath them.

Let's not give him a reason to look around then, she thought.

She ran back to the cave, remembering her mussels. She collected the meager fare, promising herself that if this scheme worked, she wouldn't have to collect another mussel for the rest of her life.

But as she turned, she collided with a hard wall. It knocked her back a step, and she peered at what she'd hit.

Her eyes met the smoldering green gaze of the selkie man, whose anger radiated off his body like a heat wave.

"What have you done?" he growled. His voice carried a dark promise of a threat.

Continue reading *Stealing the Selkie's Heart*, Book 1 in The Selkie Seas series, available July 19, 2022! (https://books2read.com/stealingtheselkiesheart)

Ronan, a selkie Anchor, is used to getting his way, and he fully expects to sort out negotiations with the local sirens before war breaks out. But when his sealskin is stolen by a desperate human, peace treaties fall by the wayside as he tries to appease her and get back what's his. And when he finds out she's his True Mate, things get even more complicated. He must seduce the human to get his skin back before war reignites.

Una MacCallan, Breck's daughter, wants to save her small Scottish fishing town from the curse that befell it 24 years ago. When she comes across a newly changed selkie, she knows he's the key to helping her. But the attraction between them is hard to fight and is only a distraction.

They must race against time to break the curse even as they fight the bond growing between them. She stole his sealskin...can he steal her heart?

Stealing the Selkie's Heart (Book 1),
available in ebook and print July 19, 2022
(https://books2read.com/stealingtheselkiesheart)

For info about new releases, please join my email list (www.EllaRoseBooks.com/newsletter).

Afterword

Thanks so much for reading *Losing the Selkie's Skin*! I had a blast writing Prion and Leannán's story, and I really hope you enjoyed reading it. If you want to start a discussion about it, feel free to email me at ellarose@ellarosebooks.com. And don't forget to leave a review on Amazon and Goodreads!

If you'd like to read more about this world, you should DEFINITELY sign up for my newsletter (http://www.EllaRoseBooks.com/newsletter) to stay up-to-date on all new and upcoming releases. I've got a few short stories set in The Selkie Seas world, and you can find out more about them on my website, www.EllaRoseBooks.com/Books.

Of all the social media channels, I'm most active on Facebook (http://www.facebook.com/EllaRoseBooks) and TikTok (@EllaRoseWrites), though I'm also on Instagram (@EllaRoseWrites),

Goodreads (@EllaRoseWrites), and Pinterest (@EllaRoseWriter). My website is www.EllaRoseBooks.com. I look forward to seeing you around teh interwebz!

Acknowledgments

I am ever grateful for a God that answers promises.

This book would not have been possible without Cathy Yardley and her Rock Your Writing instruction (http://www.RockYourWriting.com)—you are worth your weight in cheese, my friend, and I can't wait to work on the next adventure with you!

Further thanks to my editor, Tiffany Tyer (http://reedsy.com/Tiffany-Tyer), whose encouragement and hard work made this book what it is. Any gaffs that you find, dear reader, is fully on me and not her.

And finally, to my friends and family who never gave up on me, even when I wanted to give up on myself. Know that I'm raising a toast in your honor now. And let us never be too old for fairy tales!

ABOUT THE AUTHOR

Ella Rose is a paranormal romance author who loves kink, ink, and cake, and hopes you do too. She is a bi-sexual author writing through a Bi-Polar Disorder lens and thinks representation and mental health matter. Her first novel, *Stealing the Selkie's Heart*, will debut in July 2022, and her latest selkie short stories will appear in Dark Rose Press's *Worlds Apart* and Dragon Soul Press's *Beyond Atlantis* anthologies. She is a member of Romance Writers of America and the Paranormal Romance Guild. You can follow her on Facebook (http://www.facebook.com/EllaRoseBooks),

TikTok (@ellarosewrites), Instagram (@EllaRoseWrites), Goodreads (@EllaRoseWrites), and Pinterest (@EllaRoseWriter). Find out more about her at www.EllaRoseBooks.com. To stay up-to-date on all things Selkie Seas, sign up for her newsletter (www.EllaRoseBooks.com/newsletter).